THE APRIL SULLIVAN CHRONICLES

# NECROMANCER
# FOR HIRE

## DARIN KENNEDY

To Jana —
The lady's name
is Sullivan!
Darin
Kennedy

64 SQUARE
PUBLISHING

ALSO BY DARIN KENNEDY

THE MUSSORGSKY RIDDLE

PAWN'S GAMBIT

THE SICILIAN DEFENSE
& OTHER DARK TALES

Art Copyright © 2012 Roy Mauritsen. Used with permission.
Cover art and book design by Roy Mauritsen
Printed in the United States of America
First Electronic Edition: Oct 2012
First Print Edition: JuL 2015

ebook ISBN: 978-1-943748-12-9
paperback ISBN: 978-1-943748-13-6

64 SQUARE PUBLISHING

Charlotte, NC

For everyone I've met along the way,
near and far,
past and present,
here and gone.

# NECRODANCE

I clean up nice. A little gel in the hair, polo shirt, nice jeans. I look like the kid brother they never had. Makes doing what I do pretty easy.

Plus, I can spot a damsel in distress from about six miles out.

Take this one. Seven-thirty on a Wednesday night, frozen food aisle, weighing options from the fine people at Lean Cuisine. The few stray cat hairs on her black jeans tell me all I need to know. If I wanted her, I could have her back at the dollhouse tonight, but her auburn hair and freckles remind me of my first girlfriend.

And I do so hate to repeat myself.

I head down to Warehouse Hardware, or as I like to call it, "The Fish Tank." I wander around for a few minutes until I see another potential.

No ring. Shopping alone in Flooring. *Kitchen Renovation for Morons* lying askew in her basket. A bit of wear on her UVA t-shirt. I'm guessing twenty-six, fresh out of grad school, moving into her first house. I sniff the air. Yep. Dumped about a month ago.

"Redoing your kitchen?"

"The backsplash." She avoids my gaze. "Getting ready

7

to sell."

"For a project that big, you might want to wait till this weekend." I point to the sign above her head. "The Labor Day Weekend sale is usually pretty good."

"I'll be all right." She glances up at me, the corners of her mouth turned up in a tight grin. "Got a coupon."

"You ever put down tile before? It can be kind of—"

"Look. It's been a long day. All I want is to walk out of here with some reasonably priced tile and not get hit on by everything with a Y-chromosome and a pulse, okay?"

Damn. I was kind of in the mood for Italian.

"No problem."

I head down the center aisle, meandering from side to side as I take in the scenery. I stop for a moment in Lighting where a couple is deciding which chandelier to put in the front foyer. A few seconds watching them together confirms my suspicion.

The withering looks. His fretful smile. Her eyeing the salesman's crotch. Dude hasn't given his wife an orgasm in over a year. Maybe two. I make a mental note of her hazel eyes in case I run into her somewhere down the road. I have a sneaking suspicion she'll be alone.

I pass the paint aisle and catch movement from the corner of my eye.

Ah. There she is.

The main attraction.

Straight from the gym, her baby doll t-shirt sleeves just kiss her supple deltoids. Her calves strain as she balances atop a plastic step stool reaching for a gallon of paint from the top shelf. I see it coming a good ten seconds before she starts to fall. The can just beyond her reach, she goes up on her toes, her fingers grazing the handle as the stool starts to wobble. I rush over, diving forward and catching her before that firm ass of hers can hit the concrete. Her voice cuts out mid-scream as she falls into my arms.

"I've got you."

She scurries out of my grasp and gets her feet back on the floor. Five-foot two at best, she looks up at me with a mixture of bewilderment, fear, and gratitude. She brushes a caramel-colored curl from her face. The deep blue of her eyes reminds me of an autumn sky.

"You the Warehouse guardian angel or something?"

"Something like that."

"One less trip to the ER, I suppose." She cracks a crooked grin. "Thanks."

I put on my no-fail smile. "I take it you've been down this aisle before."

Her gaze flashes downward for a second, then back up to mine. "When I was twelve, my mother took away my roller skates and told me I could have them back after I graduated from college. True story."

She's funny. I like funny.

"You know, they've got the same primer right down here." I gesture to the stack of matte white on the bottom shelf. "Something special about those on the top shelf or are you feeling suicidal tonight?"

She bites her lip, cranes her neck around the stepladder at her feet and smiles. "Hm. Not paying attention I guess."

I retrieve the paint can and hand it to her. The lid's intact but the bottom corner's crushed in. If not for me, might've been her skull.

But the night's still young.

"So, what are you working on?"

"My dining room," she says. "I was thinking red."

"My favorite color."

We talk for a couple of minutes before she glances down at her watch.

"I'd better head on. Going to put down the primer tonight so I can work on the actual painting this weekend. A lot of mid-eighties pastel to cover up." She lets her foot brush the overturned step stool. "Thanks for the save."

"Y'know, I've got some experience with paint."

She raises an eyebrow. "I'll bet you do."

"No, seriously. Back in college, I worked with a couple guys flipping houses during the summers so we could eat the rest of the year. I did all the dry wall and painting."

"All right, Bob Vila. Which brush should I get to do a twelve by twelve room?" She gestured to Warehouse's arsenal of painting implements.

"I'd use a roller for the big stuff. Looks a lot more professional, and it's faster. As far as brushes, a small one for the trim should be all you need."

"What about painter's tape?"

"Painting's all about prep. You can skip a step if you're brave, but I wouldn't recommend it. A little pre-work makes clean up a lot easier."

"Hm." Her wheels turn. "You got a minute?"

"Sure."

I help her gather everything she needs to lay a decent base coat and carry the basket up to the front of the store. She pays with plastic, then shoots me a sidelong glance as she steps away from the register.

"Here's the thing," she says. "I'm not much of a painter and you at least sound like you know what you're talking about. Want to give me a few more tips over a beer? My treat."

"Sure."

I do a quick mental check.

"How about Ed's, down on the corner?"

Four months since I last set foot in that shithole. I never become a regular at any particular bar. Hard to stay nondescript if they know your name.

"All right." She flashes me a winning grin and extends her hand. "I'm April."

Her skin is soft, but her grip is firm.

"I'm Dan."

She smiles. "You look like a Dan."

I help her carry her purchases out to an old school Volkswagen bug done up in gold and blue, then follow her to the bar. We take a couple of seats by the front window, and talk for half an hour about whatever she wants. I learn more than I ever wanted about her new one-story house and its previous owners: the pastel blue they left on all the walls, the mildewed carpet, the leaky water heater. It's all I can do to stay focused in such a target rich environment. She nearly catches me making eyes at a pair of brunettes playing pool. I'm ready to write the evening off when the conversation takes a turn.

"So, Dan, you hang around hardware stores waiting for women to fall off ladders?"

"Only on Wednesdays." I let out a chuckle. "You're lucky I was there browsing."

"Lucky? Maybe." She holds up two fingers to the bartender and shoots me a wink.

I wait until she's had a couple more beers before offering to help get the primer coat on the walls.

"I don't know," she says.

"Come on." I cock my head to the side and give her my best smolder. "It's past 8 already. You'll be up half the night if you try to do it yourself."

"But—"

"Don't worry. I'm the best." I hold up my half empty glass. "And I work cheap."

She puts up a brave front, but I can see in her eyes that I'm in. Another push and she's giving me her address. I follow her to a little bungalow on a cul-de-sac a few miles from the bar.

"Pardon the mess," she says as we come in the front door.

"Mess?" The place is immaculate. "Looks pretty good to me. You have any plastic we can use to keep the paint off the hardwoods?"

She raises an eyebrow. "Don't tell me you actually came here to paint."

I feel my mouth turn up in a surprised grin. "What do you mean?"

"Do you really want me to spell it out for you?"

I can tell from her flushed cheeks that she and the alcohol mean business. She's petite, but I hadn't pegged her for a lightweight. "I guess not."

"Give me a minute."

She steps through a door into what I guess is her bedroom. She flips on a lamp, the dim light golden as it falls through the door.

"Okay," she calls after a couple of minutes. "You can come in now."

I enter her inner sanctum, and for the first time in a couple of years, I'm the one surprised. Decked out in a red leather bustier and a black miniskirt, emphasis on the mini, she flashes me a wicked grin.

"Do you like to play games?" A riding crop rests on the bed.

"You have no idea."

I slip out of my shirt as she pulls down the covers. I move

in to take her and she shakes her head, waving her finger in my face.

"No, no, no. Got to play by the rules tonight, Danny boy."

All right. I'll play her game for now.

She slips off my pants, letting them drop to the floor, then directs me onto the bed. At her direction, I get down on all fours and wait.

She gives me a light tap with the crop. Then another, a little harder than the first.

"Have you been a bad boy, Danny?" Her sultry voice no more than a whisper, she delivers another stinging pop.

"Yes."

Another pop. "I mean, really bad?"

I grit my teeth. "Yes."

"In that case…" She scoots across the bed. She slides open the top drawer of her nightstand and gets out a pair of silk scarves. "Perhaps we need to step up your punishment."

"Wow." Even I'm surprised by the nervous laugh that escapes my lips. "Do I need a safe word here?"

She raises her eyebrows. "Do you really want one?"

I lie back on the bed and give her my hands. She straddles me and ties one wrist to the headboard. I resist as she reaches for the other hand.

"What's the matter, Dan? I thought you liked games." She leans forward, her breasts straining against their red leather prison. "You're not afraid of me, are you?"

What the hell. She'll have to untie me at some point, and then it'll be my turn.

As she secures my left arm with a knot that only a boy scout should know, I notice a change. The smile is gone, but the storm in her eyes has come to life.

She rolls off me and somersaults to the foot of the bed, sticking her landing like an Olympic gymnast. "So. Whatever shall we do first?"

Her words send chills through me, but not the kind I had expected.

"Come on, Dan. Tell me what you want." That devilish grin of hers comes out for an encore performance. I wish it hadn't.

"I think the real question here is what *you* want."

"That's better." She sits at the foot of the bed, just out of reach. "For now, I suppose, I want you to think."

I feel my heart accelerate. "Think about what?"

"I'm guessing you're already thinking about it." She rises from the bed and goes into the next room. The bowie knife in my pocket might as well be in the next state. I struggle at the tight silk binding me to the bed until she returns.

"Don't bother. You'd have to break a couple of bones in each hand to get out of those knots." She stares absently out the window and sips at a glass of red wine.

"I think there's been a mistake." I try to catch her eye. "You see, I—"

"Oh, there's no mistake." She takes another sip of wine. At least I think it's wine. "I had a very interesting conversation a couple of weeks ago with a gentleman named Robert Davis. You may remember him. He was all over the news back in July. CNN, Headline News, MSNBC. He was even on Larry King if I remember right."

"Yeah, I heard about that whole thing. What does it have to do with me?"

"Mr. Davis is in a lot of pain, Dan. A lot of pain. To lose a daughter like that…"

"I don't know what you're talking about you crazy bitch.

14

I—" My voice catches in my throat as she jabs me in the gut with the riding crop.

"Be nice, Dan. You're in a precarious position to be calling people names."

"Sorry. I'm a little freaked out here. Whatever it is you think I've done, you're wrong." The fear in my voice actually gives me some credibility. "You've got the wrong man."

Her laugh chills my blood. "Perhaps." She walks to the closet and opens the door. The smell of freshly turned earth fills the room.

"Is he the one?" April asks. After a long pause, a voice that sounds like a comb being dragged across wool whispers a quiet response.

"Yes." The hairs on my neck stand on end. "That's him."

"Sorry if she's hard to hear," April says. "I did the best I could, but her vocal chords were damaged pretty badly."

"What the hell is going on here?" I stare into the darkness of the closet and see a hint of movement. I inhale to ask who waits beyond the shadowy threshold, though a part of me already knows. As she steps into the room, sweat trickles down my chest like cold fingers.

"Abby."

"Hello, Dan." My breathing grows raspy as her lips turn up into what used to be a smile.

"But… you're dead."

"And you would know." Abby takes a step closer. Her head doesn't sit on her shoulders quite right, sort of how you'd imagine a discarded puppet resting at the bottom of a drawer. Then again, I did take her head off with a shovel.

"One night?" Abby raises a shriveled eyebrow in April's direction.

"One night." A morbid glee colors her words. "Make the

most of it." She takes a step backward out of the bedroom, then turns and meets my gaze as she closes the door behind her.

"Sorry I can't stay. I'd love to stick around and play third wheel, but I'm guessing you two have a lot to talk about."

# Bonds of Blood

The necromancer and the vampire studied each other across the freshly dug grave. Her arms bare, April shoved her hands into the pockets of her jeans as the evening's damp chill stole the warmth from her body. In the dim light of the crescent moon, she could just make out the dark smudge at the corner of the vampire's mouth.

"I see you've already fed this evening."

"Have you honestly come down here to deliver the same old sermon?"

"Actually," April said, "I've come to talk."

The vampire laughed. "And what would we possibly have to talk about at this point?"

"Mom."

Something like concern flashed across the vampire's features, quickly replaced with a smirk. "I haven't laid eyes on the cow in years." He turned to leave.

"Alex, wait."

The vampire glanced across his shoulder. "Yes?"

"When we were kids, you couldn't keep the two of us apart. You can't spare a minute of your time to hear what I came to say?"

Alex sighed, pushing air from his lungs more out of habit

than necessity. "All right. One minute." He spun around and sat on a granite tombstone. "So, how is Marjorie?"

"She's sick."

"And?"

"Dammit, Alex. She's your mother, too. Show some respect."

"As you have always been so fond of pointing out, any ties to my previous life died the night I accepted the Gift. A little hypocritical coming down here with a crucifix in one hand and the family album in the other, don't you think?"

"Alex—"

"And as for respect, if you were any other person, I'd have already ripped out your throat, sucked you dry and left you at the bottom of this grave."

"We've already danced that dance, little brother." Her fingers rubbed absently at a scar on her neck. "Didn't go well for either of us, if you remember."

"The events of that evening, like most things between us, remain a point of contention." Alex rose from his granite perch and circled the grave in April's direction. "And speaking of events, I read in the paper about the serial killer found dismembered in North Carolina last month. Was that you?"

"I'm surprised you take the paper at whatever tomb you're occupying these days."

"My condo makes your pathetic little bungalow look like a shoebox." The vampire stretched. The pops of his vertebrae locking into place sounded like breaking ribs. "And don't change the subject. The description of the body from the article had all the earmarks of one of your hits. Particularly the chewed off ears."

"Bastard had it coming." Try as she might to hide her discomfort, the chill working its way up her spine made her shiver. "But I didn't come down here to talk about me."

"That's a pleasant change."

"Are you really going to spar with me all night? Sunrise is in a couple of hours and I've still got a day job. Let me say my piece and I swear you'll never see me again."

"Intriguing." Alex studied her face for a moment. "I've changed my mind. Let's do this. What's the latest and greatest with old Marjorie?"

"The cancer's come back. It's everywhere." A tear crept down April's face. "You wouldn't recognize her if you saw her."

"I'm not so certain. I imagine she looks like death."

April leaped across the grave, pulling a stake from a hidden sheath at her waist. The vampire sidestepped her attack with inhuman speed and snatched the stake from her hand.

"Now this is more like—"

April spun around, her roundhouse kick connecting with Alex's jawbone. Before he could recover, she charged into him, wrapping her lithe arms about his midsection and forcing the thing that was once her brother to the cold ground. The stake went flying into the darkness.

"You can say what you want about me," April said, her nose all but touching his, "but you will not disrespect our mother again. Do you understand?"

"Perfectly." The vampire flung April off him and into a jagged tombstone, then dove at her neck. She pulled a perfume bottle from her pocket and shot a spritz directly into Alex's mouth. He howled at the sky, his tongue smoking as if burned by acid.

"I hope you like my new scent. I've been told it's a little strong, but I think it smells heavenly." She jerked a small wooden cross from her belt and held it before her. The vampire recoiled briefly, then began to circle like a jackal on the Serengeti.

"You can bathe in holy water and cover yourself in crucifixes if you want." He rubbed his burned lips on his sleeve. "I'll end you for that."

"I only came to talk. If you would stop being such an ass…"

"Fine." Alex rested his back against a moss-covered headstone. "Don't you ever get tired of the whole 'scourge of the undead' role? Wouldn't you rather settle down, pop out your 2.4 kids and forget you ever knew things like me existed?"

"Every time a missing person report comes on the news, I wonder if they were my brother's latest Happy Meal. Makes it kind of hard to get into the June Cleaver mindset."

"And I'll never know why you always expect to speak with your brother at these incessant little family reunions. The night I was reborn, Alex Sullivan ceased to exist."

"That's a bold-faced lie. You try to hide your feelings, Alex, but your eyes betray you every time. Even when you were a kid, you had the worst poker face."

The vampire's stern expression melted a bit. "Like yours was any better."

"Do you remember when you got caught with that girl up in your room?"

"Which time?"

"Very funny. The one you told Mom was a visiting exchange student. I believe you said you were helping the girl with her English."

"She was an exchange student." The vampire smiled. "From the high school across town. And if I remember right, you were supposed to be playing lookout for me."

"Mom saw right through both of our bullshit. We didn't leave the house for a month."

"Maybe you didn't." The vampire's smile faded. "So she's

sick, huh?"

"Getting sicker every day."

"What do the doctors say?"

"They're not optimistic. They give her a month, maybe two at most."

"Chemo? Radiation?

"It's pointless. It's everywhere now, shutting down her liver, blocking her lungs." April lowered the cross and looked away for a moment. "Sometimes it's all she can do to walk across a room without stopping to catch her breath."

"Why tell me? Why would you think I even care?"

"You were her son, once. No matter what you say, a part of my little brother is still in there somewhere. I know that part still cares."

Alex cocked his head to one side. "So, when are you going to ask me?"

"What are you talking about?"

"Don't you think I've been through this?"

April held her silence.

"You want me to turn her," Alex said. "Stop the pain. I've heard it all before."

"I never said that."

"I'm not the only one who wears their thoughts on their face, April." He took a step closer. "It's been months since we've so much as laid eyes on each other. Now our... *your* mother is dying. Why else would you possibly contact me?"

"You call it the Gift." April spat the word. "Eternal life. Eternal damnation. Guess it depends on your point of view."

"Call it what you want. You're the one who sought me out."

"It's just... she's in so much pain." April looked away. "She asked me to do this one thing for her. I couldn't refuse."

"And what if I refuse?"

"That won't be a problem." April raised a hand above her head, then clenched her fingers into a fist. The air whistled as an arrow flew in and buried its head in Alex's shoulder.

The vampire howled in agony. "What are you doing?"

April met Alex's gaze, a cold fire in her eyes. "Only what I was asked."

Another arrow flew in from behind her and hit the vampire square in the midsection.

"Why are you—"

April threw a kick that caught Alex across the windpipe, silencing him. The sound of shuffling feet filled the air.

"What have you done?" His voice was little more than a croak.

His eyes darted back and forth as the ground around him erupted with scores of undead, some fresh enough to pass as human while others were little more than bones held together by sinew and willpower. Crawling, burrowing, dragging themselves from the earth, the mass of undead bodies surrounded April and the wounded vampire. They fell upon him, pressing his arms and legs into the unforgiving ground. A few moments passed and a hulking corpse with a longbow entered the circle and knelt at April's feet. She motioned for him to rise and join the still growing mob of reanimated corpses, then turned to face her brother.

"Pride."

The undead parted as April retrieved the stake and held it to Alex's chest.

"Always was your weak spot, little brother. Did you honestly believe I would let you within ten miles of my mother?"

The vampire stared up at her, his red eyes burning with hate. "Are you going to destroy me then, 'big sister'?"

April said nothing as she buried the stake in Alex's chest. The vampire let out a single gasp, then became still. April studied his unmoving form for a long moment, then waved a hand. The undead retreated from the two of them, forming a shambling, putrid perimeter. No sooner was the space cleared than April set to work.

Retrieving a leather satchel from behind a nearby tombstone, she laid out the various implements of her practice. From a small silk pouch, she poured several handfuls of white sand in a large circle around the vampire's body, the last of which she sprinkled in his hair and across his chest. She then retrieved a bejeweled dagger from her bag and knelt at the vampire's head. Drawing the edge of the blade along his sunken cheek, she watched impassive as black ichor trailed down his skin, a dark river of death. She caught a few drops of the thick black liquid in a small vial, then turned the blade on her own hand and added several drops of crimson to the mix.

Murmuring syllables that vanished on the air, she applied a drop from the vial to each of his hands and feet before pouring the remainder across his pale face. Using her index finger, she smeared this into the form of a cross on his forehead, the simple shape causing his skin to sizzle and pop as if afire.

She walked about his body three times as her undead audience looked on in dumb fascination, then pulled the stake from his body.

Alex sprung to his feet. "You bitch, I'll kill you for—"

April balled her fist and held it before Alex's face. He went silent even as his eyes grew wide with surprise. She waited for a moment, then relaxed her grip. Alex's body slackened.

"But… I'm not dead." He stared at her, unable to hide the awe in his expression.

"There's always a loophole, little brother."

Alex lunged for her and screamed. He pulled his hand back as if burned.

"Don't bother. As far as you're concerned, the space above that sand might as well be a brick wall."

"This isn't possible."

"It's quite simple, actually. No stake, you're good to go." April raised her hand, and Alex's arms flew up as if attached to invisible strings. "Staked, you're just another dead body." She motioned to the crowd of undead watching impassive from every direction.

"But I'm not like them." Alex peered around at the dozens of staring corpses. "Am I?"

"Competing powers and all that. I pulled the stake so we could talk." She tucked the sharpened hunk of wood back into her belt. "Truth be told, I wasn't sure it would work. That's why I brought backup."

She leaned so close to the line of sand, he could nearly touch her. "You know, Alex, for someone who always prided himself on the home court advantage, you should have known better than to meet a necromancer at the heart of a graveyard."

"But why?"

"Mom. She made me swear that her son would no longer prey upon the innocent." The words caught in April's throat. "With her last breath, she made me swear. The fact that you even considered her dying wish was to become like you is an insult to her name."

"I see." Alex sat at the edge of his invisible prison and rested his face in his hands. "What comes next?"

"I thought of a dozen different ways to do this. I went with the quickest and least cruel." She sat next to him, careful not to disturb the sand keeping the vampire from her neck, and checked her watch.

24

"Sixty-two minutes."

"Till sunrise." No hint of question colored his words.

"Put it out of your mind." April faced the growing pink in the east sky. "Let's enjoy this last hour, you and I."

# SOLSTICE

I really don't have time for this.

Three years without so much as a parking ticket and now I'm stuck on the side of the highway with blue lights in my rear view mirror.

Tonight. Of all nights.

The trooper knocks at the passenger window of my Volkswagen Beetle. I take a deep cleansing breath before I press the button and roll down the glass.

"Can I help you, officer?" For a moment, it crosses my mind that I could probably pull off "sexy" a bit easier if I wasn't dressed like G.I. Jane.

"Good evening, ma'am. Do you have any idea why I pulled you over?"

He's about my age, twenty-seven tops. Not too hard on the eyes. Too bad he's got on his no-bullshit face. This might be a little rough.

"I saw your headlights come on when I passed you under the bridge. You followed me for half a mile and when you flipped on the blue lights, I got off the road."

"Do you have any idea what the speed limit is on this stretch of freeway?"

"I believe the last sign I saw said 65."

"And do you know how fast you were going?"

"I'm assuming… faster than 65?" I flash him my best smile. It bounces off him like he's from Krypton.

"I clocked you going 87, ma'am. Where are you going in such a hurry at two o'clock in the morning?"

"If you want to know, I'm up against… a deadline."

I say a prayer that my little pun doesn't come back to bite me later.

His flashlight blinds me as he runs the beam across my face.

"Have you been drinking this evening, ma'am?"

He really needs to cut it with the ma'am shit.

"No, sir." I almost succeed at keeping the venom out of my voice.

"License and registration, please."

"Listen.I know you're just doing your job, but you don't understand–"

"License and registration. And while you're at it, step out of the car."

Right. Like I'd be able to explain the dagger strapped to my hip.

"I'm not sure that's the best idea. You see, I'm already running late for this thing and…"

His brow furrows. I can already see him mentally digging in his heels.

"Ma'am, I'm going to say it one more time. Step out of the car."

"I'm sorry about this." He sees me reach for the gear stick and goes for his weapon. I gun the motor, as much as Josie's little motor will gun, and drop the car into first. My tires bark as I jet back onto the highway, having to perform evasive maneuvers to keep from getting creamed by the SUV flying up my tailpipe. I half expect the back window to shatter from Dudley Do-Right's peashooter, but instead he rushes back to his car and pulls onto the highway, blue lights flashing and siren wailing. I'm running on empty, it's after 2 a.m. on a Tuesday night, and the D.C. traffic gods still fill the road with transfer trucks.

Oh well. No one ever said this job would be easy.

***

Great. Longest night of the year, and this chick pulls a drive away. Now I get to file all kinds of paperwork over a stupid speeding ticket.

"Dispatch, I'm going to need back up on Interstate 66 heading east, currently at mile marker 72. In pursuit of a late model VW Beetle, gold and blue, license plate JOSIE-81. Driver is a lone female, late twenties, possibly armed and dangerous."

The radio crackled to life. "Roger that."

"She's headed toward Arlington."

"Be advised. There's a seven car pile up two miles east of there. Do you need back up?"

"Roger on the pile up. Send back up when available."

It's getting darker out. I glance out my window at the moon. News said the eclipse goes full monty around 2:30. Thought I might actually get a chance to check it out. Instead, I'm stuck chasing this chick to God knows where.

Why is it the hot ones are always nuts?

***

Finally. Exit 75. Now it's just Wilson down to Memorial and I'm in. Except I've still got Dudley back there coming on strong. He has no idea what awaits him if he doesn't turn back now.

I suppose you could have said the same about me a few

years back.

*"Keep this to remember me by."*

The last words Julian said to me till last night. And I did it. Kept that damn orb of his all nice and safe through three states and five apartments. Bastard.

I jerk the wheel to the right and race down Memorial Drive toward Arlington National Cemetery. Dudley's close behind, but I make it to the entrance a few seconds ahead of him. I squall to a stop and leap from Josie's warm interior, making it halfway across the fence before I hear him call after me.

"Stop," he shouts. "Come down from there, now."

Hm. Confident. I look back at him. His no-bullshit face is still firmly in place.

"Look," I say. "I don't know everything, but I know people. You're about as likely to shoot an unarmed woman as I am to vote Republican in the next election. Now put the gun down."

"Don't push me." He pulls back the hammer on his pistol.

"Fine." I drop to the other side of the fence. "Go ahead. Shoot. You won't be able to do shit against the thing I'm here to stop, but do what you've got to do."

He lowers the gun.

A little.

"What the hell are you talking about?" Somewhere between incredulous and concerned, his tone leaves me fifty-fifty about whether he'll fire on me if I run.

"If we both survive the evening, I'll tell you about it over a beer. Now stop pointing that stupid thing at me and let me do what I came here to do."

He considers for a moment, then drops the pistol to his

side. "Fine, but I'm coming with you." He sprints to the fence and starts to climb over. "This crap better be for real."

"You're welcome to tag along. I can use all the help I can get. Try to keep up."

I take off at a dead sprint. The frigid air makes my lungs ache, though a different chill creeps through my body as I come to the first line of gravestones.

"*I'm going to raise an army.*" That's what Julian said. If I'm right about what he meant, we could all be in a world of shit.

It's been years since I've set foot inside Arlington, though a Google-assisted trip down memory lane got me back up to speed pretty quick. On the way here, I tried to guess where Julian would go. Arlington House would afford him a good view and be easy to defend, but if I know his style, he'll head straight for the Tomb of the Unknown Soldier. As I remember, that's over a half mile south of here. These boots may be good and warm, but I'd be better served with my old pair of cross trainers.

Any other night, the full moon would make this easy, but at twenty minutes from total eclipse, I can barely see the ground at my feet. I take off across the grass and curse myself for a fool. This crap has been all over the news for weeks. Lunar eclipse on the winter solstice for the first time since the 1600's and I didn't even think twice when Julian of all people shows up at the bar wanting to talk about old times.

I'm such an idiot. There are no coincidences. Especially where he's concerned.

"Ow!"

Dammit. Tombstone ricochets off my shin, and I can't even be mad. Hell, they're even laid out all military like and everything.

Come on, April. Can't afford mistakes tonight.

I keep running, though even with my pride in full swing, I can't avoid a bit of a limp. I feel blood trickling down my leg beneath my jeans. A panicked thought echoes through my subconscious. Even if I'm right and Julian's here and even if I find him in time, how the hell am I supposed to stop him? He taught me everything I know about this shit.

Well, almost everything.

I pull the Janus dagger from its sheath and hold it before me as I run. It should get brighter the closer I get to Julian's mystical doodad. Not to mention, it sheds a little light on the path. Don't need a matching scar for the other shin.

"Hold up!" Dudley shouts from behind me.

He sounds a little winded, but he's gaining on me. I'm guessing he spends some serious time on the treadmill.

All right, April. Got it. He's cute. Now, stay on task.

***

Looks like she's hurt. She's limping, but still staying ahead of me, at least for now.

Why did she have to bring me here of all places? Haven't been back since we put Jonny in the ground. Mom keeps begging me to bring her out to the grave…

Figure that out later. Remember the job.

"Hold up!" I shout.

She pauses for a moment, then rabbits away as fast as that gimpy leg of hers will take her. At least she whipped out that big silver glow stick. Don't think I'd be able to track her otherwise. I'll be on top of her in just a minute.

On top of her. Come on, man. Focus.

***

The Tomb of the Unknown Soldier is straight ahead. The last

time I was here, it was all of us.

Dad.

Mom.

Alex…

Stop it. It's 2:27. This whole thing is going down in thirteen minutes and if there's one thing I remember about Julian, it's his punctuality.

"Hello, Sullivan." Little more than a hiss, Julian's voice sets my hair on end. "I thought we might cross paths this evening."

I spin around and find my former mentor atop the facade of the Memorial Amphitheater, though the thing that looks down on me isn't the man who taught me seven years ago or even the man I traded shots with last night. Julian always had an aura of death about him, but the musty stench that permeates the air despite the howling wind is almost more than I can stand.

And I raise the dead for a living.

"Hello, Julian."

"And here I thought I was so cryptic." I believe the expression on his face is supposed to be a smile. "Yet again, the student rises to meet the teacher."

"Don't do this. The people buried here have earned their rest."

Julian cocks his head back and laughs. "The people buried here are warriors. I merely come to give them another chance at glory."

"I know you, Julian, and even you aren't so delusional to believe that anyone here longs to reenter this world of pain, especially under your thumb."

"How many times must I teach you this same lesson? Once raised, the undead want only one thing. To please their deliverer."

"Oh. So now you're some kind of savior. Never figured you of all people would develop a messiah complex."

"And how many have you raised in the seven years since you left my side, Sullivan? Do not dare to speak to me from whatever imagined moral high ground you think you hold. I have followed your 'career' with much interest. Mere months ago, you raised an entire graveyard to handle a personal matter. You've taken money in exchange for your rather unique services, lured men to their doom with your seductive charms, not to mention you've all but advertised our existence to the world at large. You may see me as a despot, but in my eyes you are little more than a whore with delusions of grandeur."

I clutch the dagger in my hand to keep it from falling. I'll have to sort out later whether my hand trembles more out of fear or rage.

"Give me the orb, Julian."

Even in the waning light, I can appreciate the incredulous look in his cadaveric eyes.

"You can't be serious. Surely you know who holds the upper hand here."

"Hands in the air."

The new voice comes from my rear. Dudley.

"You're trespassing after hours on government property. Put down the knife and get down on the ground." He shifts his attention from me to Julian, directing his sidearm at my once mentor. "As for you, come down from there."

"Why, Sullivan. You brought the police. How... quaint."

I hold my position and watch as Julian brings the orb up from within his robe and begins a whispered chant.

The cop pulls back the hammer on his weapon. "Come down from there or I will fire."

Hm. Dudley's holding up pretty well for what I'm

guessing is his first encounter with bad mamma jamma. Impressive.

"Officer. Listen to me. I—"

"I told you to get down on the ground."

"Stop and look around you, man. Can't you see what's happening here?"

In a show of good will, I rest the dagger on a nearby tombstone.

"What's your name?"

"Lieutenant McLaren."

"No. Your name."

He hesitates. "Gavin."

"Gavin, turn around and forget you ever saw any of this. This is my fight."

His gaze returns to Julian. "What is he?"

"Your conquerer, little man." Julian chuckles. "And before you consider wasting your bullets, understand that all the steel and gunpowder at your command are of no consequence this evening." A barely perceptible smile blossoms on my old mentor's face. "But feel free to fire if you must."

I check my watch. 2:31.

"Listen, Gavin. In about nine minutes, all hell is going to break loose in this place. Julian isn't kidding when he says you can't hurt him. He's invincible to pretty much anything this world can throw at him."

Gavin lowers his weapon. Holy shit, a man that listens. "How are *you* going to stop him?"

I kick my foot up, flipping the dagger up from the tombstone, and snatch it from the air.

"This blade is not of this world."

"Clever, clever." Julian raises the orb. It shimmers dark violet in his skeletal hand. "Perhaps some additional players to keep our little drama interesting."

All around me and Gavin, hands rip through the sod. Skeletal fingers encircle his ankles and force him to the ground. He cries out, a potent mix of fear and agony. As he goes down, he gets off a couple of shots. I see Julian's shoulder recoil from the impact, but he doesn't fall.

Not this night.

I rush to Gavin's side and slash at the skeletal wrists and arms that hold him in place.

"Who are you?" he shouts, his voice garbled as bony hands encircle his throat. "Why is this happening?"

"Reader's Digest version?" I free his neck and go to work freeing the rest of him. "Gavin McLaren, April Sullivan, necromancer for hire."

"Necromancer?" He glances up at the monster that used to make me tea on Thursday nights, a wicked grin plastered across his desiccated face. "And who... what is that?"

"The thing atop that building was once a man named Julian LaMorte." I free his legs and help him to his feet. "He taught me pretty much everything I know."

I meet his gaze and head off his next question. "You don't want to know what I know."

A flash of violet light from the corner of my eye sends my body into motion before I can think. I shove Gavin out of the way as a bolt of eldritch energy strikes the grass at our feet. The blast leaves nothing but a barren patch of charred earth.

"We've got to get out of here." I cast about for cover. "He's getting more powerful with each passing second."

He catches my arm. "And you were going to face him alone. Are you crazy?"

It's corny, but I feel a little charge from his fingers on my sleeve. "Shut up and move."

I grab his hand and run for cover. The small copse of trees to our left looks substantial enough to shield us from view. I glance at my watch. Seven minutes. Dammit. My plan didn't account for anyone but me and Julian tonight.

"Plan," I mutter aloud with a chuckle. "That's a laugh."

"What do we do now?" Gavin asks.

"You stay down and out of sight. Julian is my business."

"What does he want?"

"No time for twenty questions. I don't know what he wants but what I do know is if I don't stop him, he's going to take that little orb of and raise this whole damn place. If that happens, a century and a half of dead soldiers are going to hit D.C. like an undead tsunami."

"You're kidding, right?"

I feel my cheeks getting hot. "Have you already forgotten that a corpse just reached up out of the ground and tried to kill you a minute ago?"

Gavin looks into my eyes, his defiance melting into a frustrated grunt. "Noted."

"Now stay here. If you see anything other than me moving, run like hell."

\*\*\*

"*April Sullivan*," she said. "*Necromancer for hire.*"

And she wasn't kidding.

I watch from behind the enormous tree trunk as she runs for the amphitheater. She's lucky LaMorte and that – I can't believe I'm even thinking this word – "death-ray" of his isn't too accurate.

She weaves between the tombstones like a trained quarterback and despite the limp, she makes good time. I lose her as she takes the steps, which is good, because I have a feeling whatever is causing the rustle in the leaves behind me is going to require all my attention.

In various states of decomposition, three corpses dressed in service uniforms head for me as fast as their shuffling feet will bring them. Their medals shine in the fading light, even as their stench assaults my nostrils. I spin to my left and find another pair of shambling undead headed my way. I raise my Beretta to fire into the nearest one, then lower and holster my weapon. I'm packing one of the best pistols known to man and I'd be better off with an axe.

Hell, a stick.

Before the two groups of undead soldiers can combine their lines and surround me, I dive between them and take off through the grid of marble tombstones. I count at least a dozen more, all homing in on me like heat-seeking missiles. Fortunately none of them seem able to move faster than a slow stumble. I glance up at the moon and watch as the last bit of light vanishes and the surface of the moon turns blood red.

I circle in a wide arc through the cemetery and work my way back around to the Tomb. As I get close to the enormous marble monument, a thought crosses my mind.

"Where are the guards?" I mutter. "This place is guarded 24-7."

As if in answer, a stern whisper from behind states, "Post and orders remain as directed."

I turn to find a man, or at least a thing that was recently a man, stumbling toward me, its rifle aimed at my chest. It's dressed in the uniform of one of the tomb guards.

"Post and orders remain as directed."

Its head cocked to one side, I half expect to hear the funky break from the end of Michael Jackson's *Thriller* video.

"Stay back. Just passing through."

Its hissed whisper grows louder. "Post and orders remain as directed."

What does it want me to say? "Roger?"

The thing that was once one of America's best and brightest charges me, his finger squeezing the trigger again and again. Luckily, the honor guards don't come loaded for bear.

"Sorry about this."

I lean into the running corpse, grabbing it about the midsection and flipping it onto the ground behind me. I'll handle the fact that I just apologized to a corpse tomorrow.

If there is a tomorrow.

The undead guard falls in a heap behind me and I charge toward the amphitheater. There, atop the majestically columned building, April and the creature she calls Julian are facing off. The dagger in her hand is shining like a star, though its light is nearly engulfed by the deep purple energy coming off the jeweled globe in her mentor's hand.

"No doubt about it, Gavin." I glance across my shoulder as the undead guard gathers himself for a second rush. "You are in way over your head this time."

\*\*\*

I race up the stairs of the amphitheater. The Janus dagger makes short work of the two locked doors between me and the roof.

Three minutes.

I clamber across the dilapidated shingles toward the front of the building. The wind is picking up and more than once threatens to pitch me from atop the amphitheater. I come upon Julian's hunched form. In my younger days, I might have hoped I could surprise him, though I know better than to count on such a pipe dream these days.

"Stop this, Julian," I shout over the screaming wind.

"Before it's too late."

The low chant stops as he turns to face me.

"Ah, Sullivan. You were ever the most dramatic in my long run of students." He shakes his head in mock concern. "Do you not understand? From the moment you returned my orb to me, this die was cast. All your posturing aside, in two minutes an army will rise, and nothing you do or say will stop that."

"Can't blame a girl for trying." I clutch my own talisman, the one Julian gave me all those years ago, and pray it will afford me at least a measure of protection as I charge at him with dagger raised. I half expect to see at least a glimmer of fear in his eyes, but instead he looks on me with measured patience, as if I were no more than a misbehaving child. Then, as I draw within striking range, his unencumbered arm shoots out and his rough fingers encircle my throat.

Dammit. He was never that fast before.

"And so it ends, Sullivan. Pity. It didn't have to come to this. Take comfort in knowing that as you die, you will no longer be alone but another soldier in my risen army."

I bring the dagger to bear against Julian's skeletal arm, slashing at the leathery sinew that holds the bones of his forearm together. I might as well be trying to cut a hunk of granite with a butter knife.

I died once. Buried alive – not the best way to go. It really sucked. It felt a lot like this.

Darkness invades from the corners of my vision, and I'm pretty sure it's not just the eclipse hitting its stride. My lungs burn as I struggle for air. With what's left of my vision, I watch as Julian raises both his arms to the sky. The orb in his hand overlies the moon just as the eclipse becomes complete. My last thought is what happens to a necromancer's soul when she dies.

The crack of gunfire echoes through the cemetery.

Julian's hand jerks as the bullet strikes him just below the wrist, sending the orb flying into the darkness. Seconds later, the sound of shattering crystal pierces the night.

Through my oxygen-deprived fog, I follow Julian's gaze and find Gavin atop the Tomb, his sidearm smoking in the cold night. All around him, better than two dozen shambling corpses fall to the ground. I can't help but laugh.

"Stopped by a single bullet," I croak from between Julian's crushing fingers. "How quaint."

"No." Julian hurls me to the rooftop. My head smacks the rough surface with a sickening crack. Stooping over me, he takes the platinum and jade bauble from my hand and vanishes in a flash of dark iridescence. He reappears a moment later atop the Tomb next to Gavin, my talisman held high above his head.

Gavin is about to pay the ultimate price for crossing a necromancer.

\*\*\*

No good deed goes unpunished.

The thing April calls Julian appears beside me atop the Tomb. He's on me before I can move. His breath smells like a carcass left out in the sun and his face is more like a mask than anything that used to be alive. From the corner of my eye I get a glimpse of the object he's holding. A shallow crescent of metal and stone, it shimmers in the night with a sickening green glow.

"Centuries." Pus sprays from his mouth and I fight the urge to gag. "Centuries waiting for this night, and you, insignificant gnat of a man, have ruined it."

I get off two shots into the void that used to be his chest before he swats the gun from my hand.

"Your weapon may have served to destroy my orb but I imagine you will find I am far more durable."

His weapon goes dark, as if absorbing the light at its surface. He raises it above his head and begins a slow chant. I suddenly feel very cold.

"Please," I get out as the world starts to go black. "Don't."

"Fear not." He smiles. "I will ensure your death is anything but quick."

I fall to the top of the Tomb, my paralyzed eyes staring unblinking at the crimson moon above as each breath comes harder and harder. I hear the clang of metal on stone as darkness continues to creep over me. Then I see a flash. A face. Then nothing.

\*\*\*

I watch in horror as Julian hits Gavin with The Darkness.

A shiver runs through me. Before Julian taught me that trick, he let me feel a fraction of the power he's throwing now. Pain, cold, suffocation. As one of the few people on the planet who's felt what he's feeling, I'm surprised when Gavin lasts almost a minute before his body falls to the cold marble. So brave, so stupid. I told him to stay out of sight.

But if he had, we'd all be dead.

I creep to the edge of the amphitheater, fighting against the vertigo that threatens to send me falling to the stones below. I hold the dagger by the blade, say a quiet prayer to a God I stopped believing in years ago, and let the blade fly.

Watching the knife flip end over end, a fist of ice grips my heart as I watch Gavin's only hope of survival ricochet off the marble at Julian's feet. My once mentor chances a glance at me, his body shaking as he chuckles at my failure, and misses the rush of movement from behind him. A form in military dress rushes the platform, scoops up my dagger and leaps at the Tomb.

Julian spins and raises my talisman, but not before the soldier is upon him. Their fight lasts mere seconds, ending as the mysterious soldier drives the shimmering dagger deep into Julian's chest.

I rush back down the stairs, but by the time I make it to the platform again, everything is still. Two dozen corpses lay splayed about the area, the energy of the orb and Julian's invested life force no longer animating their long dead limbs. Julian lies unmoving by the white marble tomb. I can barely make out the outline of Gavin's body from my limited vantage.

"Gavin!" I climb to the top of the tomb and check his pulse. Thready and rapid, he somehow survived Julian's assault. I hold my cheek to his mouth like I learned from a CPR course in a different lifetime and feel his feeble attempts at breath on my skin.

"Live, dammit." I close my mouth over his cold lips and force air into his lungs. "Live."

I breathe life into his still form for fifteen minutes until the next guard shows up. He doesn't know what to do, poor kid. Probably expected to show up and watch a piece of marble for a couple of hours. Instead he finds a scene out of *Army of Darkness*.

"Hey, kid," I shout. "Go get help."

"But, my post—"

"Screw your post. This man is dying. Get the paramedics here, now."

He runs and I keep pumping air into Gavin's lungs. A couple of minutes pass and he coughs as he tries to raise his head from the cold marble.

"Am I… dead?" His voice is little better than a whisper.

"Not if I can help it."

He tries to sit up.

"Where's Jonny?"

"What are you talking about?" I hold his shoulders to the stone, keeping him still. "Jonny?"

"My brother, Jonathan. He was here."

"I have no idea what you're talking about. Julian was about to kill you. I threw the dagger and missed big time. The only reason you're still alive is one of the guards finished the job and saved your ass."

"No." I hear the rattle in his breathing as he coughs up a mouthful of blood. "It was Jonny. I saw him." He turns his head to the side. "Just like the day we buried him eight months back."

"Your brother was buried here?"

He nods. The effort takes all he has.

"But anyone that Julian raised would have been under his thrall."

"It was Jonny, dammit." I'm surprised by the fire in his voice. "He was holding your blade. He saved me."

What Gavin is saying is impossible.

But I deal in the impossible.

"Look. I need to check on something. Are you all right?"

He coughs out another mouthful of blood, looks up into my eyes, and puts on his best semblance of a smile. "I think so."

I pull off my jacket despite the cold and fold it into a pillow for his head. "I'll be right back. Don't... die or anything."

He chokes out a chuckle and nods again.

I climb down from the white marble slab and inspect the bodies along the flat surface. There's what's left of the reanimated tomb guard, the other recently undead in various stages of decomposition, and one lone soldier in full dress uniform. I flip over the body and gasp. His face a younger version of Gavin's, the chest full of medals tells the story of a man who found his true calling. I don't know what all the ribbons mean, but anyone with that much fruit salad wasn't just punching the clock.

Clutched in his dead man's grip, the Janus dagger still holds a faint glow, though its business is done for the night. I retrieve it and return it to its sheath, then reach around the body's neck and pull out the dog tags.

"McLaren, Jonathan P., 255-04-5319, O Pos, Catholic."

"Damn." I glance up at the tomb. "Gavin was right."

\*\*\*

The ICU smells of ammonia and copper as I head for room 18. Gavin's nurse is adjusting an IV drip as I enter. He lies there on the hospital bed in a nest of wires and tubes, surrounded by machines that monitor his every breath and heartbeat.

All I see is his smile.

"Feeling better?"

"I am now." His voice is reminiscent of a frog with a bad cold. "Good to see you."

I smile. "Good to be seen."

"Is everything…" He glances at the doorway to make sure no one is within earshot. "You know, done?"

"Everyone and everything is back where they belong. Not sure what the tomb guards are going to file in their report, but that's a problem for another day."

"And Julian?"

"Gone. He channeled most of his life force into the orb you destroyed. The kind of mojo he was trying to work with last night doesn't come cheap. Once it was shattered, the rest was just a matter of time."

"I killed him?"

"He was dead long before you came along." I glance out the window at the rain pelting against the glass. "Hell, before I came along in all the ways that count."

"And Jonny?"

"At peace. I made sure of it."

"So, what's next?"

"Not sure." I sit on the bed next to him and take his hand. "I just wanted to come by and thank you for saving my life."

"Right back at you."

I feel my cheeks get hot again, but this time for a different reason. "When are they going to let you out of here?"

"Another day or so." He glances at the door again. "I'm feeling stronger by the hour, though it's nothing they're doing. I'm not sure they know exactly what to make of me. As you can guess, I left out a few parts of my recent history."

"Smart. They'd probably move you to a different floor if you told them everything. You know, the one with the rubber rooms. Plus, I'm pretty sure they don't cover necromancer attacks in medical school."

"So." A sad smile invades those hazel eyes of his. "This is your life?"

Crap. Here it comes.

"This is it. It's what I do."

He squeezes my hand. "Cool."

Despite my best efforts, I let out a nervous laugh. "You mean all this stuff doesn't scare the shit out of you?"

"It does, but I think I could get used to a little bit of fear." His gaze falls to the hospital linens. "When I get out of here, I'd like to hear more about, you know, how you got into all this. Maybe… over dinner?

"Why, Officer McLaren. Are you asking me out?"

He smiles. "Yes, ma'am."

"Two conditions, then."

"Tell me."

"Number one. Cut the ma'am crap."

"Roger." He laughs. "And the second?"

"Do you think you can take care of a little speeding ticket I got last night?"

# Class Reunion

If life is nothing but a big spinning wheel, then the axle at the center of my life is death.

The big "D" is as much a part of my life as ledgers are for accountants or teleprompters for politicians. Hell, it's right there on my business card: "April Sullivan – Necromancer for Hire" below a row of arcane symbols inscribed by a friend who knows more about the dark arts than I will ever care to learn.

On any particular day, I may raise someone long dead from their "eternal" slumber or put yet another deserving soul into the ground. It's just what I do. Like a doctor pulling together a hundred different pieces of information before prescribing what he hopes to be the correct medicine, I interpret life and death. And when it comes time for such decisions, it's almost always just that, a matter of life and death. Death in all its myriad forms is as inseparable from my experience as the oil under a mechanic's fingernails.

And even harder to scrub away.

Why then do I dread the next ten steps so much? If I had a dollar for every corpse I've seen in my twenty-eight years on the planet, I could take the year off and enjoy a long sabbatical on some remote Caribbean island. Who knows? Maybe Haiti. Could show the natives what a real zombie looks like.

But I digress. And that's the whole point isn't it? To forget for a moment where I am and why I'm here?

The death of a stranger, for most of us, means nothing. The news every night tells of the latest soldier killed in a war we shouldn't be fighting, entire villages destroyed by drones piloted by kids sitting in air-conditioned rooms thousands of miles away, countless terrorist attacks both at home or abroad, genocide after genocide, tsunamis, earthquakes, even meteor strikes. We take it all in, then flip to ESPN to see how our team did the night before like nothing happened. Do we truly feel any of it anymore? Seems to me the average American is far more interested in who's getting voted off some stupid island or being fired from some make-believe job each week. Meanwhile someone's elderly grandmother breathes her last, all alone in a cold bed three houses down the street. Hell, even I've grown more than a bit callous over the years.

Much like the Colorado River has left a slight indentation on western geography.

This? This is different.

This is personal.

"You okay?" Gavin squeezes my arm. "You're awfully quiet. We don't have to do this, if you don't want to."

"I can handle it." I'm so glad Gavin agreed to come with me to this. I can't imagine a worse fate than being stuck alone at a funeral as all the former jocks and cheerleaders reconstruct their high school existences around the casket of one of their own. "Just stick with me, all right?"

Gavin pulls me in tight. "Won't leave your side."

I haven't run into nearly the number of classmates I expected to, but in each of their eyes, I find the same two emotions no matter their outward façade: sadness and shock.

Sorrow about losing someone they once knew ten years ago in another life? Possibly.

Fear about the number of days they themselves have left to walk the earth? Definitely.

The line for the coffin is down to about fifteen people when a long-forgotten voice speaks my name.

"April?" I turn my head to the right and fight the urge to retrieve the Janus dagger from my purse as a far-too-perky-for-a-funeral blonde charges me, her arms raised as if she expects a hug. "April Sullivan, right?"

Damn. "Hello, Kitty."

"Wow." Kitty crosses her arms before her. "It's been a long time."

"Ten years and change, right?"

"I guess you're here for Bill's viewing."

Poor Kitty. Still about as dumb as a box of hair. I file through the top twenty or so snarkastic responses that beg to fly from my mouth, but settle for, "Bill and I were pretty tight our junior year. It was the least I could do."

"Can you believe it?" Kitty says. "He was only twenty-eight years old."

"He died of a pulmonary embolism." This far more welcome voice from behind us fills my heart with much needed joy. "Blood clots don't differentiate by age."

Kitty and I turn and find Bradley Young coming down the narrow hallway. In an Armani suit and shoes you could eat ice cream off of, he's barely aged a day, though he's not the beanpole I remember. Boy's been hitting the gym. A transfer in our senior year, Brad was more or less responsible for me graduating high school.

Without killing someone, that is.

"Wow, it's good to see you, Brad." I pull him into a tight

embrace and the ten years since we last spoke evaporates like dew on a July morning. "How's residency treating you?"

"They're letting up a bit this year. The hospital only works me twenty-five hours a day instead of twenty-seven."

"Great seeing you, Brad." Kitty pounces on him like a lioness on the Serengeti. "You look fantastic."

"Thanks." Brad cuts to his left and steps around Kitty. "So, April, you've obviously been keeping up with me. What have you been up to?"

I give him the standard answer of the evening. "I've been working as a consultant the last few years."

"Ooh. That sounds so official." Kitty's gaze stays focused on Brad like a twin set of laser beams. "What kind of consultant, April?"

My face grows hot. I'm not embarrassed about who I am or what I do, but "I raise the dead for a living" never goes over all that well in polite company. I flash a nervous glance in Gavin's direction and before I can get out another syllable, he's on it.

"Hi, Brad. I'm Gavin McLaren."

"Brad Young." He shakes Gavin's hand. "April and I were good friends back in the day."

"Good to meet you," Gavin says, and the funny thing is, he means it. Most guys would be jealous of the tall, muscular, good looking, best friend from high school doctor, but not Gavin.

God, I love this man.

I take Gavin by the elbow and pull him into me. "Brad's a third year surgery resident at Georgetown." I do my best to ignore Kitty's repeated attempts to get in on the introductions. "We spent a lot of time together my senior year of high school. I'm not sure I would've studied a lick the whole year if it weren't for him."

Brad laughs. "And I would've hit a lot less parties if it weren't for April."

Kitty clears her throat and offers Gavin her hand. Her wrist hangs a bit limp for my taste. "I'm afraid we didn't get introduced. I'm Kitty Hawks."

"Gavin." His lips pucker as he struggles to suppress a laugh. "Nice to meet you." Gavin always picks up on the subtle nuances of names, though there's nothing subtle or nuanced about this one. Before he laughs in her face, I return the save.

"Congratulations, by the way, Kitty. I heard through the grapevine that you and Gary finally tied the knot." I incline my head to one side and will my eyes to fill with interest. "How does it feel not being a Snellenger anymore?"

"Daddy always used to say, 'once a Snellenger, always a Snellenger.'" Her gaze drifts to the floor. "It's weird coming home and not having him around."

"Oh." Wow. I actually feel bad for Kitty Snellenger. I'm not certain, but I believe this is a first. "When did your father pass?"

"Oh, daddy's not dead. He's just… finishing up some time away."

"I heard about the trial," Brad says. "Only a couple more years till he's out, right?"

"Summer after next." She turns to me. "I guess you haven't heard. Dad was put away for embezzlement three years ago. Got his sentence dropped to five years by turning state's evidence on some of his partners. Gary and I are doing just fine, but there are no Beamers for Kitty these days." She looks down at her wrist, a department store watch in place of the diamond-encrusted Cartier she wore our senior year. "We're doing just fine."

"I'm… so sorry, Kitty." I don't know which surprises me

more: the fact that the words come out of my mouth, or that I'm pretty sure I mean them.

"The line is moving." Gavin gestures in the direction of the polished gray box with silver handles surrounded by flowers. A box that holds the body of the first boy I ever kissed. "You ready?"

"Do I look ready?"

Kitty waves to someone in the back of the line and skitters off to meet them, leaving Brad, Gavin, and I standing in the doorway. The casket rests at the end of a long, rectangular room. Atop the closed lower half of the box rests a bouquet of Easter lilies. Always the optimist, Bill once told me they were his favorite flower. He said they represented hope, peace…

Rebirth.

Stop it April. What you're thinking is out of the question. You're here to pay your respects, not to stir up trouble.

Or anything else.

I pause a second to take in the fragrance of the lilies, then step around the large bouquet and look down on all that remains of William Alan Barrett. Though I've prepared for the moment for two days, I can't hold back a gasp as I find an unfamiliar face in the gray casket. His hair cut close to the scalp in an almost military style, gone are the curly locks my fingers always used to find in the dark of our favorite movie theater. His forever-closed eyelids hide those brilliant blue irises that always reminded me of an Alaskan glacier. His skin dusky and pale, those lips that were always turned up in mischievous grin now form a thin, straight line held in place by undertaker's glue.

"Oh, God. Bill…" I reach down and grab his cold hand. The chill of his skin works its way up my spine. I stand there for a long moment without a clue of what to say. I hear the voice of my mother as if she were standing next to me telling me to close my eyes and say a prayer. Funny thing is, the last time I said anything to God was at her funeral a year ago. I don't remember what I said, but no comfort came from on high that day, or any day since for that matter. I certainly don't expect that to change today. Truth is, if you expect nothing, you'll never be disappointed.

"You okay, April?" Gavin's rich baritone rips me back to the present.

"I didn't think it would be this hard. We dated for the second half of our junior year till his mom found out. I wasn't exactly what she considered a "desirable" girlfriend back then. I haven't so much as looked Bill up on Facebook since we graduated." I stroke my fingers along the cool, smooth cheek that I remember as always warm and rough with stubble. "I guess I always thought I'd get the chance."

"That's funny." Another voice. Female. Familiar, but only a little. Filled with anger. "From what I remember, you're the kind of woman who makes her own opportunities."

I turn to face what is sure to be another familiar face but can't quite place the woman that stares at me from not five feet away.

"Excuse me," I glance at Gavin, then back at the woman. "Do I know you?"

"You don't remember me." She glances around the room, meeting one incredulous stare after another. "I get the homecoming court over in the corner forgetting me, but you, April?"

I look closer, and in my mind replace the woman's bleach blond hair with brown curls, the stick-thin body with curves just shy of overweight, the overdone makeup with the round tortoise-shell glasses that were in style fifteen years back.

"Janey?"

"I go by Jane, now, but yes." She steps closer. I feel the hair on my neck rise. "We only rode the bus together every day for the first eight years of school."

"I'm sorry. It's just, you look so... different."

"I would certainly hope so. Otherwise the twenty hours a week I spend at the gym are a big fat waste of time."

"Hi, Janey." Brad makes a cautious wave in her direction. "I haven't seen you since graduation."

"Haven't thought about me since graduation, don't you mean?" She glances around the room. "None of you have. None of you, that is, except Bill there."

I pull close to her and bring my voice to a whisper. "I'm not sure what you're trying to accomplish here, but this isn't the time or place."

"Quiet, Sullivan." She tilts her head to one side. "We'll have words in just a moment."

"I think we should talk now." I grasp her wrist and attempt to pull her toward the exit. "Let's take this outside."

She jerks her hand free and backs away from me. "Like I'm going anywhere with you. You may look all innocent in your conservative little black dress, but other than your boyfriend there, I'm guessing I'm the only person in the room who knows your little secret."

"My...secret?" I glance at Gavin. "I'm not sure I know what—"

"Don't try to bullshit me, Sullivan." Quiet gasps hit my ears from multiple directions. "I know the truth. I was there. Third grade? Behind the gym?"

"Third grade?"

"It was a sunny afternoon as I remember. Our bus had broken down and we were waiting near the gym for a new bus. You got bored and wandered off behind the gym to climb around on the air conditioning unit. I was about to join you when a robin smacked full speed into a closed window just above your head and fell at your feet, its body broken and lifeless. Sound familiar?"

I feel the color drain from my cheeks.

I was eight years old the first time my particular set of talents expressed themselves. I remember the moment as if it were seconds ago. The average elementary school girl would have screamed bloody murder, but that day, when the dead bird fell at my feet, a different emotion came over me.

A calm.

No. More than that.

A certainty.

I crouched down and picked up the bird's still form, its feathered neck turned at an angle not consistent with life, and a new emotion filled my mind. Neither revulsion nor sorrow, this feeling of sheer wrongness wiped everything else away. More than anything, my eight-year-old mind railed at the unfairness of it all.

"It's not your time," I muttered again and again, as I stroked the dead bird's feathers. "It's not your time."

To this day, I'm not certain how long I huddled there behind the gym cradling the dead robin, but I still remember the quickening of my heart when the bird stirred in my hands. The twitch of its foot. The flutter of its wing. I screwed my eyes shut as a white-hot tsunami of emotion rushed down my arms and into my hands. When I again opened my eyes, the bird rested on my finger staring at me, very much alert and very much alive. As it flew away, I tried to convince myself it had merely been stunned by the impact with the glass, but somewhere deep inside, I knew the truth.

The very truth Janey Wolfe seems poised to scream to

the world.

"I'm not certain what it is you think you remember from two decades ago, Janey, but whatever it is, this is not the place to discuss it."

"We're not going anywhere, Sullivan. I was counting on you being here tonight, and now that we're all together again…" She glances over at Kitty who reentered our airspace a few seconds ago. "So, Kitty. You asked April here about her consulting career. Would you like to know what she does for a living?"

"Janey." The heat returns to my cheeks. "Don't."

"It's Jane, you manipulative little bitch." She returns her attention to Kitty. "Do you want to know?" She casts her gaze around the room. "Do all of you?"

Bill's mother, Lorraine Barrett, who has done her best to stay out of the drama, breaks from the receiving line and joins the still growing circle of Bill's friends and family. She catches my eye and a flash of recognition crosses her face.

"Ladies," she says. "This is my son's funeral. What the two of you do outside these doors is none of my business, but in this room you will show some respect."

I inhale to apologize to a woman whose last memory of me is no doubt a scrawny teenager wearing too much makeup standing in her front yard and bawling her fool head off. Before I can speak a word, Janey takes a step forward.

"Respect? You want to hear about respect? I've been seeing your son for going on six months and unless I miss my guess, I'll bet you've never even heard my name."

Mrs. Barrett's gaze drops to the floor, then rises to meet Janey's crazed grin. "And you would be wrong, dear. I know exactly who you are."

"Do you?" As Janey takes another step toward Mrs.

Barrett, Gavin maneuvers himself between the two women.

"That's quite enough." Gavin raises a hand, and for a moment, Janey stops in her tracks. "I'm Officer Gavin McLaren with the Georgetown Police Department. Cease and desist, or I'll have to place you under arrest for disturbing the peace."

Janey studies Gavin for a moment, then shoots a smirk in my direction. "Heard you were seeing a cop, Sullivan. Doubt he brought his sidearm to a funeral, though." She slides a snub-nosed pistol from her purse and levels it at Gavin. "Now, if all of you will just stay back, April and I have a few things to discuss."

The phones come out around the room, and I have no doubt that my face will be all over Twitter, Facebook and Tumblr in a matter of seconds. But that's not the worst of it. Not by a long shot. I hold my tongue, not sure what to say or even feel. Though ten years have passed, the realization that the first boy I ever loved has been sharing a bed with a lunatic kills me.

I just hope it doesn't kill someone else before the night is over.

"How dare you?" Mrs. Barrett steps around Gavin and comes face to face with Janey, the gun between them pointed at her belly. "You weasel your way into my son's life, make him miserable for months, and then show up at his funeral with foul words and a gun?"

"And of course, your son, the impeccable William Barrett is completely innocent in all of this." She leers around the room. "Someone like Bill wouldn't take a girl home and bed her after their first date. Wouldn't lead her on, dropping by at all hours of the night when he was feeling horny."

Mrs. Barrett raises her hand to slap Janey, but I catch her wrist before she can bring her three carat diamond across Janey's face.

"Don't give her an excuse," I whisper.

"What would you have me do, then?" Mrs. Barrett's eyes narrow in anger. "I will not stand here and let her desecrate my son's memory."

"Neither will I." I pull her away from Janey, placing myself between her and the gun's muzzle.

Brad steps forward and pulls Kitty behind him. "Stop it, Janey. There's got to be a better way to handle this."

"And you would know, wouldn't you Mr. Big Shot Doctor." Her gaze wanders back and forth between Brad and Gavin. "How cute, trying to one up Sullivan's cop boyfriend. Some things never change."

I sense Brad bristle at Janey's words and can almost feel her finger tighten on the trigger. "Thanks, Brad, but if you want to help me, get Kitty out of here and let me handle this."

"Yeah," Janey says. "Let April handle this. Matters of life and death are her specialty."

I shoot my gaze at Brad as he inhales to say something no doubt brave and possibly ill advised. "Just go. I'll be all right."

"But—" Brad says.

"Go. Now." Brad escorts Kitty from the room, and the majority of the crowd follows suit. I turn on Janey with a practiced grin, doing my best to keep her attention on me. "I know what you want, Janey."

"Oh, do you?" Her eyes gleam with malice.

"This isn't my first rodeo, as you know more than well."

She smiles. "Shall we get to it, then?"

"Two conditions."

"Demands, April? In case you've forgotten, I'm the one with the gun."

I cock my head to one side. "Do you want to talk to him," I whisper, "or don't you?"

"Fine. What are your conditions?"

I motion around the room. "Everybody else leaves. This is about you, me and Bill."

"I'm not going anywhere." Gavin rests a hand on my hip. I can feel his body close behind me, his chest rising and falling against my shoulder blade.

"I didn't figure you would." I squeeze his hand in mine. "Help clear the room?"

"Of course." Before he can make a move, Mrs. Barrett steps forward.

"This is my son's funeral." She glares back and forth from Janey to me. "Whatever this thing is between the two of you, I'm not going anywhere either."

I bite my lip. "Mrs. Barrett, please. She has a gun. This is going to be a whole lot harder with you still here."

"Then it's going to have to be harder." She crosses her arms and sets her jaw as she turns to Gavin. "Now, Officer McLaren, if you will get the rest of these people to safety, I'd like to get this travesty over with so I can finish saying goodbye to my son."

"Will do, ma'am." It takes Gavin but a couple of minutes to clear the room, the few wannabe journalists remaining far more interested in recording everything for posterity than saving their own skins. Upon his return, it's just the five of us: Gavin, Janey, Mrs. Barrett, Bill and me.

"Now what?" I glare at Janey, imagining thirty different ways I could put her down if I didn't have to look out for Gavin and Bill's mother. "You've officially pissed all over Bill's last moments and, like it or not, have my full and undivided attention. Tell me what you want."

Janey brushes a stray lock of blond hair from her eyes. "The same thing as you. To say my goodbyes." She crinkles her nose and shoots me a subtle wink. "If you catch my drift."

Mrs. Barrett steps forward. "To say your goodbyes? Bill said you were crazy, but I had no idea—"

Janey fires a round into the ceiling. "Watch your mouth, mommy dearest. I'm not the president of your fan club either."

"Whoa. Everyone calm down." I hold Gavin back with one hand while raising the other in an effort to placate the crazy woman with the gun. "Mrs. Barrett, I let you stay here out of respect for your son, but for God's sake, please let me handle this."

Mrs. Barrett looks away, but other than a quiet sigh, she doesn't say another word.

I walk to the coffin and look down on Bill's still face, wiping away a tear before I turn to face Janey and the pistol directed at my navel.

"Before we go any further, we need to discuss some ground rules."

"We're not discussing anything, Sullivan. I'm betting every person your cop friend escorted out of here is calling 911 as we speak. This place will be swarming with his buddies any minute now, so stop your stalling and get to work."

"To work?" Mrs. Barrett looks at me. "What is she talking about, April?"

Even now, I can't tell if Mrs. Barrett knows my name only from tonight or if she remembers me from ten years back. When she knew me before, my hair was dyed black to match every article of clothing I owned, I kept my skin paler than Edward fucking Cullen, and I was definitely not as good with the whole "not being a colossal pain in the ass" thing.

Surprise, surprise. This little necromancer went through a goth phase.

"Mrs. Barrett, there's something about me you don't know. Something that makes me a bit… different."

I glance at Gavin. His eyes haven't left the pistol in Janey's hand since he reentered the room. If I can just get him that chance.

"Oh for Christ's sake, Sullivan." Janey joins me beside the casket, keeping one eye on Gavin and the other on me and Mrs. Barrett. "What darling April here is trying to tell you is that she can raise the dead."

Mrs. Barrett's brow knots above her eyes. "Raise the dead…"

"Yes, Lorraine. Raise the dead. I have one of her cards right here." Without taking her eyes off any of us, Janey slides her free hand into her purse and flings a familiar business card in Mrs. Barrett's direction. "And it's not just a hobby. Oh, no. This is what she does for a living." The corners of her mouth turn up in a smirk as she leers at me. "Guess the crazy bitch your son was dating a few months back isn't looking so bad anymore."

Mrs. Barrett stoops and retrieves the card from the ground. She studies it for a moment, then looks up at me, an all-too-familiar fear in her gaze. "April, is this true? Or even possible?"

I hesitate for a moment, then nod.

"So you came here to raise Bill? To actually… say your goodbyes?"

"No." I glance at the lilies atop the casket and decide that half a truth is better than no truth at all. "I came to pay my respects. That's all."

"Come off it, April." Janey steps closer to me, still keeping all three of us in her line of sight. "I know you keep your business quiet, word of mouth only and all that, but people talk."

"That's enough. It's clear you know what I can do. Let's get down to business."

"What is it you want her to do?" Mrs. Barrett asks.

Janey half-shrugs, keeping the gun pointed at my midsection. "I want 'Little Miss Necromancer' here to bring Bill around for a few seconds here so I can tell him thank you for dumping me like yesterday's garbage. His little restraining order made it a little difficult to get in touch there at the end."

Mrs. Barrett lets out an unamused hmmph. "Surprised someone like you would let a stupid piece of paper keep you from doing anything."

"Shut up, bitch." Janey returns her attention to me. "Tick tock, April. Time is running short. You can keep up the innocent act about why you're here, but I'm guessing you've got everything you need to do the deed right there in your purse."

I can feel the curve of the talisman my teacher gave me bulging through the leather at my side. Custom made from platinum and jade, Julian said the gray metal represented my moral core while the green stone at its center represented life coming from death. The thought of the cool metal crescent in my hand is intoxicating. The rush of raising someone is like a drug, a fact I keep in mind every time I do my job. I've met more than one of my kind who have fallen prey to the addiction and been forced to put down each and every one of them. A slippery slope, I've managed to stay on the straight and narrow so far.

My fingers brush the Janus dagger as I slip my talisman from my purse and I consider briefly bringing a very different tool of my trade to bear. Electricity screams along the nerve endings of my hand as I hold the glowing crescent talisman above my head.

"What is that?" Mrs. Barrett asks.

"The thing that's going to make your little boy dance one last time." Janey laughs. "Still think she came just to pay her respects, Lorraine?"

"Shut it, Janey." I bring my talisman close to my chest,

the green glow surrounding the platinum crescent growing brighter with each passing second. "This is my talisman, Mrs. Barrett, a focus if you will. The power is all me, but it helps to have something bring it all together. Sort of like a lightning rod."

"And that would make you the lightning." Mrs. Barrett's face shifts back and forth between curiosity and horror.

"Lightning," Janey says. "All flash and bang, but no staying power."

I shoot her my coldest stare. "I'll show you power."

My eyes slip closed as I draw upon the forces that surround us all but only few can perceive. My every thought focuses on that same bird I raised behind the school gym so long ago. Even after all these years, it's the robin I visualize every time I prepare myself to do what I do. The warmth of its still red breast. Its splayed wings. The flutter of its heart in my hand the moment before it flew to rejoin the sky. Since that day, I have returned movement, speech, even breath to countless dead, but only on that occasion did I feel that I returned life. Though I'm grateful that absolute power over life and death seems beyond my grasp, a small part of me remembers how it felt when that bird came to life in my hands and flew away. That part of me, the part I always ignore, still craves that feeling, the rush of new life, the conquering of death.

I glance across my shoulder at Mrs. Barrett. "Forgive me," I whisper.

She inhales through her nose and shakes her head sadly as I return my attention to her dead son. My first task, the lips. The dead I raise don't necessarily need to breathe since they're, well, already dead, but I've found that most find it disconcerting if they awaken with their mouth sewn and glued shut. Plus, Janey wants to have words with Bill.

As do I.

I draw the tip of my talisman across his closed mouth and undo the undertaker's work. I do the same for the eyes and am relieved when the lids stay basically in place. Staring death in the eye is never easy. When the eye in question once looked at me across a field of daisies like I was the only flower in his line of sight…

"Get on with it," Janey moans. "We don't have all night."

I ignore Janey's derisive words and press the point of my talisman into the pad of my left thumb until I draw blood. Yep. Hurts every time.

"April." Gavin draws close as a drop of my blood lands on the white rose at Bill's lapel. "Are you all right?"

"Just assembling all the ingredients." I touch my bloodied thumb to each of Bill's eyelids and then to his pale lips, parted now as if he is about to speak. I remember a time when running my fingers across those lips sent a very different charge through me.

I lean across his body and whisper a single word.

"Breathe."

A moment passes, then a second, then Bill's chest rises and falls like a bellows. His eyelids flutter like a pair of pale moth wings, then open. At first dead and dull, his pupils grow dark, almost alive. No color returns to his cheeks, as his blood has been replaced with embalming fluid, but even the minimal movements of his face bring back the boy that taught me how to swing dance.

"April?" His voice, once deep and resonant, comes out like steel wool on sandpaper. "April Sullivan?"

"Hello, Bill."

"What are you doing here? What's happening?" He glances to his left and right, his eyes growing wide with terror. "Where am I?"

"I'm sorry, Bill. I never meant for this to happen. My hand was forced."

"Enough small talk, you two." Janey steps up and pushes me aside, her gun still leveled at my belt. "Your job is done, Sullivan. Now be a good girl and go stand with your boyfriend over there."

"Boyfriend?" Bill says. "What is this? What's happening?"

"Bill." Unable to hold her silence any longer, Mrs. Barrett rushes over to the casket. I'm half afraid that Janey's going to shoot her, but even a psycho knows not to get between a mother and her son.

I hope.

"Bill. It's me. Your mother."

"Hey, Mom." The confusion in Bill's eyes continues to grow. "Is everything okay?"

"Yes. No. I mean… I never thought I'd get the chance to…" Mrs. Barrett breaks down into tears. "Oh, Bill…"

"All right." Janey pushes Mrs. Barrett aside toward the foot of the casket. "If everybody is done with the tear-filled reunions."

"Jane?" Bill instinctively takes in a breath he no longer needs. "What the hell are you doing here?"

"That's the thanks I get? I arrange a way for you to say your last goodbyes, and that's the first thing you say to me?"

"Goodbyes?" Bill examines his surroundings a second time. "Casket. Flowers." His jaw drops open, and though impossible, his cheeks seem to grow a shade paler.

Janey spits out a derisive laugh. "And finally, our class salutatorian figures it out."

Raising his head from the pillow to gaze past the arrangement of flowers atop his casket, Bill stares at me. Through me. Into me.

"I'm… dead, aren't I?"

I bite my lip. "Not at the moment."

"You did this?" he asks.

I nod. "There's a few things I never told you back in the day."

He notices the gun in Janey's hand. "You crazy bitch. You made her do this."

"Watch your mouth."

"But why?" Bill asks.

Janey's lips turn up in a smug smile. "You don't get to die on me that way, Billy Boy. We have unfinished business."

Bill's dead eyes focus on her. "Always did have to get the last word, didn't you?"

"Actually, I want you to have the last word." Janey purses her lips. "Apologize."

Bill stares incredulously at Janey for a moment, then bursts into laughter, the sound like the last wheezes of a cancer patient choking on his own blood.

"What's so funny?" Janey puts the gun in Bill's face. "Stop laughing at me."

"Or what?" Bill says. "Your little pistol there won't do much good against a dead man."

"You're right." Janey tilts her head to one side as she levels the pistol at Mrs. Barrett. "On the other hand, I could arrange a more permanent reunion for you and your mother."

Bill's gaze shoots to his mother, his eyes wide. "Leave her out of this."

I sense Gavin tense and grab his arm before he can act.

"Don't," I whisper. "I've got this."

Janey strokes a finger down Bill's chest. "Now, say something nice or your mom's going to be in a whole lot of pain."

"Don't listen to her, Bill," Mrs. Barrett says. "The police will be here any minute."

"And that's quite enough of your mouth."

As if in slow motion, Janey levels the gun on Mrs. Barrett. Seconds before, the situation seemed poised to resolve itself, but my assessment left out one simple fact.

The woman holding the pistol is batshit crazy.

The crash of Janey's gun leaves my ears ringing. Mrs. Barrett crumples to the ground. The splotch of crimson at her waist grows to the size of her fist in a matter of seconds.

"No!" Gavin is almost on top of Janey as she spins and fires another round. The bullet catches him in the thigh and Gavin goes down in a pile of muscle and finely tailored wool.

Janey levels her pistol at me. "You going to make a move on me too, Sullivan?"

"In a matter of speaking." My fist closes around the talisman and in a guttural voice a single word falls from my lips.

"Now."

Faster than Janey can think, Bill's dead arms wrap around her, seizing her wrists. The gun discharges twice into the ceiling before it drops to the floor. Janey's eyes fill with terror.

I pull in close, and whisper into her ear. "Four people in the room, and not only do you fail to shoot the necromancer holding the magical doodad that can raise the dead but you take your eyes off the reanimated corpse that's under her thrall as well? I knew you were a bit dim, Janey, but how stupid can you be?"

"Make him let me go, April." All malice gone from her voice, the whiny little girl I remember from elementary school makes a reappearance.

"Don't worry." I hold the talisman up before her eyes, the viridescent glimmer of the metal pulsing in time with my heartbeat. "You'll be gone soon enough."

Gavin drags himself over to Mrs. Barrett's bleeding form. Finding her unconscious, he rolls her onto her side and does everything in his power to keep her alive.

"She's bleeding out, April. Do something."

I return my attention to Janey. "You caused this problem. Only fitting you be part of the solution, you know?" I stroke the point of the talisman down Janey's cheek. "Close the karmic circle and all that?"

"Wh-what are you going to do to me?" Janey asks.

"Remember what I did with the bird?"

Tears well in her eyes as she shakes her head from side to side. Before she can utter another sound, I shove the tip of my talisman between her ribs. Her eyes grow even wider as the talisman begins to pulse to a different heartbeat.

Hers.

"Life is a balance, Janey." I watch as her blood flows down my talisman. The light emanating from the metal goes from green to a deep purple. "All of us are born. All of us die. An even trade."

"Please don't kill me," she sputters.

I ignore her. "Any other transaction comes at a cost. Blood for blood. Life for life." I pull in close for a second time. "Do you understand?"

"Please."

A part of me almost enjoys hearing her plead.

"April," Gavin cries out. "What are you doing?"

I glance over at him. The world around us appears blood red. "Putting things back the way they should be."

I pull the glowing metal crescent from Janey's chest. A train of gore connects them like some grisly umbilical cord. The whispered words come to my lips from nowhere like they always do. The room grows cold even as the power begins to build.

"But you can't do this," Gavin shouts. "Stop before it's too late."

I spin and glare at him. "She'd kill all of us without a second thought. Why should I show her mercy?"

Without a thought, Gavin answers. "Because that's who you are."

Then another voice.

Bill's.

"He's right, April." His voice is almost calm, a stark contrast to the iron grip he maintains on Janey's arms. "I don't know how you've done what you've done, but I can see what you plan to do. There's got to be another way."

"But your mother."

"Is still breathing." Mrs. Barrett raises her head up from the carpet. "I feel it, April, what you're trying to do. I don't want it. I don't want… *her* in me."

"But, you might die. I can't have that on my conscience."

"All of us are born." She echoes my own words back at me. "All of us die."

In the distance, I hear sirens. Help is on the way. Gavin keeps one hand over his bleeding thigh and the other on Mrs. Barrett's belly wound. Janey, still conscious, grows paler by the minute. And Bill, poor Bill, stares at me from beyond the grave with a potent mix of sorrow, anger, and regret.

"If you really want to put things the way they should be, then release Janey and let the authorities take care of her."

I think about his words for a minute, then release my grip on the talisman. Bill's hands fall from Janey's arms, his deathly grip apparently the only thing that held up her unconscious body. She falls to the floor and I'm left the only one in the room still standing.

"Good," Bill says. "You let her go. Now, let me go."

"But I never got to—"

"Just say it now." Somehow, the embalmed corpse of the first boy I ever kissed manages to put on a warm smile. "Better late than never, right?"

I try without success to hold back the tears. "Goodbye, Bill." And with that, I allow the talisman to go dark. Bill's head falls back upon the pillow, the momentary interruption of his eternal rest over at last.

"April," Gavin whispers. "Help."

I rush to Gavin's side. He's doing his level best to stem Mrs. Barrett's bleeding, but he's getting weaker himself as the pool of blood beneath his thigh continues to grow.

"What can I do?"

"You think that crescent thing of yours and my belt will work as a tourniquet?"

I pull his belt from about his waist, quite cognizant of the fact it's the first time I've done that, and wrap the leather about his thigh a few inches above the wound. I slip my talisman beneath the leather and twist the cold metal in my fingers. My efforts manage to stanch the flow. Though Gavin's skin is pale and clammy, he looks practically ruddy when compared to Mrs. Barrett. Her skin the color of faded linen, her breaths grow shallower by the moment.

"She's dying, Gavin." I squeeze her cold hand. "And other than disobeying her last wish, there's not a damn thing I can do about it."

"Don't worry." Janey's voice sends an icy spike through my heart. "You'll all be joining her in a moment."

I jerk my head to the side and meet Janey's crazed gaze. A few feet from where I left her and propped up on one elbow, she's retrieved the gun and now has the business end trained at my head.

"Not so stupid now." She pulls back the hammer on her pistol. "And I won't make the same mistake—"

A deafening boom fills the room and Janey's form crashes into the foot of Bill's coffin. The acrid smell of gunpowder fills my nostrils.

"Is everyone okay?"

Gavin and I follow the voice to find a uniformed policeman standing in the doorway. His sidearm still held before him, smoke pours from the barrel. Gavin's eyes light with recognition. Must be one of his buddies.

"Kyle," he says. "We need the EMT's here like yesterday."

"They're right behind us."

I turn my attention back to Mrs. Barrett. Without bringing the energies at my command to bear, all I can do is hold pressure on her wound with one hand while I keep Gavin's tourniquet tight with the other.

"It can't end like this for her. Not like this, with her dead son lying five feet away."

Officer Kyle steps across me and takes control of the tourniquet, allowing me to give Mrs. Barrett my undivided attention.

"Hang on, Lorraine." I whisper in her ear. "Help is on the way."

***

"Funny how I always seem to end up at the hospital when you and I get together." Gavin slides into his shirt, his discharge papers resting on the edge of the hospital bed. "Thanks for coming to pick me up."

"Least I could do. If it weren't you in that bed, it'd be

me."

If I was lucky.

"Still," he says with a grin, "no one I'd rather have sitting at the foot of my bed."

Something about Gavin's smile always brings out the best in me, or more accurately, puts the darkness in its place for at least a moment or two.

"Mind if we swing by to check in on Mrs. Barrett before we go?" I ask. "There's a couple things I need to say to her."

The nurses taking care of Gavin won't let him walk out under his own power, so I end up pushing him in a wheelchair down the hall toward the step-down unit where Lorraine Barrett has spent the last couple of days. From what I understand, she lost a few feet of bowel and required several units of blood to bring her around. However, all signs point to her pulling through. I've kept up with her condition every few hours, but haven't had a chance to talk to her yet. She's either been asleep or too medicated to talk the times I've visited.

"Hello, Ms. Sullivan." Mrs. Barrett's nurse, Joanne, runs into Gavin and me at the door to the ICU. "Here to see Lorraine?"

I give her a quick nod. "How's she doing?"

She smiles. "See for yourself."

Joanne leads me back to the room. As we enter, she pulls back the curtain revealing Mrs. Barrett awake and sipping on a protein shake.

"You're awake." I park Gavin's wheelchair and move in to give her a hug.

"Careful, dear," she grunts. "I'm still pretty sore."

I pull back and sit at the foot of her bed. "I'm so sorry about what happened, Mrs. Barrett. If I hadn't shown up for the viewing, none of this would have happened."

She fixes me with a no-nonsense stare. "If you hadn't come, who knows what might have happened." Her mouth shifts into a regretful smile. "You weren't the lunatic that brought a gun to a funeral home, remember?"

I stroke her leg through the white hospital blanket. "From what I hear, you're going to be just fine."

"That's what they tell me. Even lost a couple pounds." She shoots a mischievous gaze at Gavin. "Though it's no weight loss plan I'd ever recommend."

"I'm glad you're going to be okay, Mrs. Barrett," Gavin says.

"Thank you, Officer…?"

"McLaren."

"Officer McLaren." Her eyes shoot back and forth between Gavin and me. "I owe you both my life."

"Just doing my job, ma'am. Wish I could've done more."

"How's your leg?" Mrs. Barrett asks.

Gavin shakes his head. "Nothing's broken, thank God. Bullet went straight through my thigh and clipped one of the big veins down deep. Doctors say I'll be up and at it again in a month or so if I do my therapy."

"We've all got therapy coming, I would imagine." Mrs. Barrett shifts her gaze to me. "And you, April. Are you… all right?"

"I am, now that I know you're going to make it through."

A coughing fit overtakes Mrs. Barrett for a moment. She clears her throat and glances over at Gavin. "Officer McLaren, may we have a moment?"

Gavin glances over at me, and at my silent nod wheels himself out of the room.

"I have a confession to make, April." Mrs. Barrett says.

"Truth is, I didn't think much of you when you were dating my son back in high school."

"I sort of picked up on that. Bill's speech when he broke up with me didn't sound much like anything I'd ever heard him say." My cheeks flush with heat. "I know it's ten years too late for it to matter, but you have to know that I loved your son. I loved him more than anything... and he loved me too."

"I get that." Her eyes drop. "As it would seem is evidenced by the events at his funeral, my Bill didn't always have the best taste in women."

My stomach turns at her words. "Now that's not fair. I—"

"April," Mrs. Barrett says. "Stop. This is hard enough as it is."

"All right." I swallow the bile at the back of my throat. "Go on."

"Like you said, it's all my fault that you and Bill didn't work out back in high school." She looks away. "At the time, I just couldn't see him ending up with someone like you."

"Someone like me?"

"All dark hair, pancake makeup and eye liner. My little boy was going to end up with the perfect woman and you, my dear, just didn't fit the bill."

"But—"

"Please. Let me finish." She clears her throat. "Bill always could pick 'em. I can't recall the one time he brought anyone home I thought was worth a damn." Her eyes narrow, even as her lips turn up into a hint of a smile. "I suppose I wanted to let you know that in at least one case, I may have been a little... quick to judge."

"Mrs. Barrett, I—"

She puts a finger to her lips and motions for me to come

closer. As she takes my hand and pulls me down toward her lips, she whispers, "Call me Lorraine."

"All right, Lorraine." I squeeze her hand. "Is that all?"

"Just one last thing." She glances at the sliding door leading out to the nursing area. "That cop you're dating? He's a lucky man." She shoots me a subtle wink. "Don't you ever let him forget it, understand?"

Great. The last time this woman saw me before tonight, I had far too much black mascara streaked down my face from crying over her son and here I am again, brimming with tears.

"Thank you," I manage to get past the oversized lump in my throat.

"No, April. Thank you." Her eyes begin to well with tears as well. "It's rare that a mother gets a second chance to say goodbye to her child. As awful as it was, I had that chance. To see Bill one last time, to hear his voice, look into his eyes. You can't know what that meant to me."

"Actually, I do know. This is what I do for a living, remember?"

"True." She takes my hand in hers and gently strokes my fingers. "A piece of advice from a woman with a few more years and several more grey hairs than you?"

I smile. "Of course."

"This… necromancy stuff. Like you said, it's what you do, but never forget it isn't who you are. Don't get so wrapped up in death that you forget to live your life, understand?"

"Yes, ma'am."

"And that young man waiting in the hallway? I see that same intensity in his eyes that I used to see in Bill's when your name would come up." She squeezes my hand. "Between you and me, in ten years, I never saw that look in Bill's eyes again. Not until two nights ago, that is." She turns and looks out the window at the bright blue Virginia sky. "Death may be the final destination that awaits us all, but life is a journey, and not one meant to be travelled alone."

# Solomon

There was a time when the mere mention of my name would loose the bowels of any man who heard the three simple syllables, when entire cities would empty upon the rumour I might pass their streets a month hence, when kings and paupers alike understood the appropriate respect due one who was ancient when their ancestors had yet to come down from the trees. I often question if the infuriating lack of deference in these more "modern" times represents a willful refusal to recognize true power or is merely the blissful ignorance of the teeming masses.

In any case, I miss the old days.

I glare across the scrying table at one of the reportedly more capable men in my employ, a technological expert named Henri whose apparent sole reason for existence is his tacit understanding of these magical screens that seem to open doorways to anywhere in the world with but a few... what does he call them?

Keystrokes.

When last I roamed the earth, keyboards were situated firmly in the realm of music: pianos, harpsichords, pipe organs. In my time, I've witnessed Mozart eke true beauty from stricken ivory and ebony, listened to Chopin wax poetic without uttering a word, marveled as the great Mussorgsky resurrected the paintings of a departed friend's posthumous art exhibition with nothing but the notes and chords of a box filled with steel strings and felt hammers. Henri can summon all of these wondrous works to his "monitors" with the simple push of a button. The "Net" he calls it. But this net of his is not so well made. It may bring the music, but it cannot bring the musician, the composer, the soul behind the melodies that capture generations.

And if anyone comprehends matters of capturing souls…

"Ahem."

With this simple clearing of his throat, Henri becomes a perfect illustration of my rumination. If I had not been assured this ferret of a man was "simply the best man for the job," I would already be feasting on his warm entrails rather than giving him one last night before the ruin that awaits in the morn.

"Yes, Henri?" If the derision in my voice registers in the man's puny skull, he doesn't let it show. "What is it?"

"The Sullivan chick. She's still coming and somehow managed to disable the cameras on the 27th and 28th floors. We last saw her on 25, but she could be anywhere by now."

"I have yet to understand why you insist I be concerned about this wench. She is but a lone woman." I taste bile at the back of my throat. "And a mere slip of a girl, as I understand."

"I wouldn't underestimate this one, boss. She's taken out some heavy hitters recently." He taps a few buttons and a face appears on the largest of the screens. Freckled and fair, her curly auburn locks impart an aura of innocence I suspect she left behind long ago.

"April Sullivan, 'Necromancer for Hire' according to the various business cards we've recovered. Family all deceased, her brother apparently more than once. All reports state his final passing was at the hand of his estranged sister."

"Fratricide. How delicious."

"Sullivan is implicated in paranormal related hits all over the world that have occurred over the last three years. In fact, all evidence suggests that she was the one who faced LaMorte at the height of his power during last winter's solstice."

"LaMorte is an overconfident fool."

"I believe you mean 'was' an overconfident fool, boss. There have been multiple reports of the necromancer's activities in the months since. LaMorte, not so much."

A buzzing at the back of my skull compels me to glance across my shoulder, but when I look, there is nothing there but a dark, empty corner.

Quite empty indeed.

"Then it would seem that yet again the natural cycle of things has prevailed." I crack my knuckles. "The student becomes the master, even as the master ages, fades into obscurity, and eventually passes on to the next realm." I reach out one long finger and catch Henri by his collar, pulling him close. For the first time in our short interaction, I see an appropriate amount of fear in the man's gaze.

"Would you care to know, Henri, how it is that I have survived as long as I have?"

"Of… of course, boss."

"I trust no one and teach no one anything." I pull him even closer and enjoy the shock on his face as the stubble on his chin singes under the heat of my breath. "Never forget that a secret shared is a secret no longer." I run my tongue across the jagged row of teeth that has ended the lives of more men than I can even fathom, and allow myself to smile. "I've never found myself bested by a student for I've never taken one."

"That's smart, boss." Sweat rolls down Henri's face. "Real smart."

"Henri, a simple request."

"Yeah, boss?"

"Do not call me that."

"Do not call you what, b—" He cuts the word short as fire flashes across my visage, then very quietly asks. "What should I, err, we call you, then?"

I have been called many things through the centuries. The Hunger that Hides in the Darkness. The Black Scourge of Europe. He Who Cannot Be Sated.

"A simple 'my lord' shall suffice."

"Sure thing, my lord. I can… Wait. There she is. On 29 and heading for the stairs."

Henri points to one of the black and white monitors where I finally get a glimpse of this Sullivan woman who has a score of grown men squealing like frightened schoolgirls.

In other times, one of my favorite sounds.

Armed with nothing but a crossbow and what appears to be one of the lesser Elder Blades tucked at her side, she creeps down a half-darkened hallway. At first, she seems ignorant of the camera eye observing her every move, but then I notice it. The slow deliberate nature of her movements. The angle of her body as she makes her way toward the door. The telltale flicker of her eyes in the direction of the lens.

She knows we are watching. The cow is putting on a show.

"Henri."

"Yeah, boss… my lord?"

"I have had enough of watching this fragile twig of a woman outsmart the small army you and the others have assembled at my behest. I wish you to gather your men, find the wench and bring her to me." I pause a moment. "I want her alive."

"You want this bitch still breathing?"

"She is of no use to me dead. The essence of one who can bring to ground one such as LaMorte is a prize I cannot brush aside."

"But the sacrifice. She's coming here to stop it. To stop you."

Another smile finds its way to my lips. "What fearful symmetry. She comes to stop the ritual, and in doing so becomes the final piece of the ceremony that will bind me to this world she seeks to protect."

Henri glances at his bank of monitors. "She might have something to say about that."

I gesture to the hallway. "We won't know until you bring her to me. Now, go and fetch the girl." As Henri scurries for the door, I shout after him. "Wait. Before you go. Show me the sacrifice."

Henri goes to one of his three keyboards and taps at the lettered buttons for a few seconds. A moment later, a screen to his left switches from a view of an empty hallway to a room three floors above our heads. A circle surrounding a thirteen-point star fills the space, at each point a child, bound, gagged and blindfolded. The smallest of the thirteen cries uncontrollably, his body bobbing with each sob.

I can almost taste him.

"Send the ten best men to guard the children. Take the rest with you."

Henri all but runs from the room, leaving me alone, the space lit only by the dozen screens that fill the back wall.

"You may come out now." I motion to the dark corner that before piqued my interest. "The only thing empty about this room is your hope of leaving it alive."

I wait the space of two breaths before the air in the corner shimmers. Slipping from her neck a familiar amulet, the woman who seconds before walked across the screen stands before me.

"I see from your choice of accessory that you have made the acquaintance of my old friend Klaus." I gesture at the amulet hanging from her clutched fist. "That ornament brought him great fortune for centuries."

She blows a lock of auburn hair from her eyes as she tucks the amulet into a pouch at her side and draws the dagger from its sheath. Even more than the amulet, I recognize her blade.

"Herr Bindlekroff, master of illusion," she says. "It would seem the biggest illusion he held was his own immortality."

I remember the last time Klaus's eyes met mine. The hatred. The cold certainty. If this girl has indeed ended him, perhaps I should reward her rather than ripping her pale body in twain.

"You expect me to believe a child such as you could dispatch a man like Bindlekroff?"

"Man?" Her eyes narrow as she passes the dagger to her fighting hand. "Bindlekroff was no more a man than you, Solomon."

In the middle ages, there was a legend that even the whisper of my name would bring me to the bedchamber of the utterer at midnight to gorge on their still living body. To hear it bandied about so nonchalantly brings a red haze to my vision, a haze I banish before it can take control. If this woman has truly bested both LaMorte and Bindlekroff, she didn't do it with brute force, but with cunning.

"Clever girl, but you will have to do more than attempt

to blind me with anger if you hope to survive this evening."

"Oh, I plan to do so much more than survive." She takes a step forward and slips into a chair. "I have come here tonight to negotiate for the lives of the children you hold three floors above our heads."

"Indeed?" I pull around a chair and sit opposite her. A folding table covered with empty coffee cups and cigarette stubs is all that stands between us. "You say you have come to talk, yet you hold in your hand the dagger of Janus."

She smirks. "My father always taught me to negotiate from a position of power."

I lean forward in my chair until mere feet separate us. I sniff the air and catch her scent. My stomach rumbles. "And you believe that eighteen inches of enchanted steel and a Chinese trinket imbued with the simplest glamour give you such power?"

"You underestimate the Janus dagger at your peril. And as for Bindlekroff's amulet, you know as well as I do it is no mere trinket. My greatest power, however, comes from knowledge."

Intrigued, I ask, "And what knowledge is this on which you stake your very life tonight?"

"What was it you said before?" Her lips turn up in an unsettling smile. "A secret shared is a secret no longer?"

Truth be told, I find myself amused by the girl's insolence. A quiet chuckle escapes my lips. "It would seem I have violated my own rule and taken a student."

"I am certain we could teach each other many lessons this evening," she says, "but I have come only for the children. Release them into my charge and leave this place and this is over. I have no feud with you, at least not yet."

"Brave words, little girl. Brave words." I lean back in the chair. It creaks under my weight. "Over the centuries, I have found that most are brave, until they see my true face. Are you quite certain you wish to see that side of me?"

"If it comes to that. At the moment, you are stalling. Will you release the children?"

"You already know the answer."

"And so the negotiations begin." She leans in, her voice shifting to a conspiratorial whisper. "If you will not release them, perhaps you will accept a challenge. A wager, if you will."

Again intrigued, I grumble, "Speak your mind."

"I propose a contest, you and I. At stake, the lives of the children, no more, no less."

"Stupid girl. I was ancient when your ancestors discovered how to make fire with two stones. You gamble with the children's lives, something that is not yours to wager. What is it that you bring to this betting table?"

For the first time, she hesitates. Her fear tastes like honey.

After a long moment, she adds, "My fealty, my life." She looks away. "My soul, in service to you."

"Your fealty I would never trust and your life is already mine, merely waiting for me to take what you gave up by setting foot in this room. Your soul, however, will more than suffice."

At the center of the circle three stories above is another, smaller circle. The ritual to again bind me to this plane requires the lives of thirteen innocents and culminates in the slaying of the earth mother. I had hoped this necromancer cow would qualify for the latter role. As I smell the life that grows within her, I can't help but smile.

"Name your challenge."

Her eyes go up and to the left, a tell that has been present since man began to walk on two feet. She's making this up as she goes. My smile grows wider.

"A battle of wits. And one last condition."

"A battle of wits?" I feel my eyes narrow. "Against you?"

"A fiend from Hell vs. a 'mere slip of a girl', oh He Who Waits for the Sunset?" She laughs. "Surely you didn't expect me to suggest a physical confrontation."

"Done, though I am curious about this final condition you propose."

"A question. When this is done and you look into my eyes, the eyes of the one who defeated you, I will ask you a single, simple question and you must answer with the truth."

"Your life wagered against a single answer. I had not taken you for a fool."

"I am no fool, Lord Solomon." Yet again, her face slides into that disconcerting grin. "LaMorte is dead and my education is incomplete. I would be your student, if but for one answer. And do not dismiss me, for you have yet to hear my question."

"Your life for a single answer. First you seek to anger me into a foolish mistake and now you attempt to lull me with flattery. Unless I miss my guess, I suspect I know which won you that amulet you hide there in your pocket."

Sullivan turns her head to one side and bats her eyelashes at me like some Parisian courtesan. "Bindlekroff may have been older than dirt, but his inner horndog was alive and well."

"And LaMorte?"

"As you said before to your underling." She runs her finger along the hilt of the Janus blade. "His overconfidence got the best of him."

"I would hear how you ended your much esteemed teacher's long and storied existence, but enough preamble. Let our contest begin."

Her brow furrows for a moment, then her face relaxes. I feel my own eyes grow wide as she returns the Janus dagger to its sheath and pulls a deck of cards from her jacket. She spreads them in her hand and lays three of them on the table.

King of hearts.

Queen of spades.

Jack of diamonds.

She returns the rest of the deck to her pocket, then takes the three cards from the table and folds them lengthwise down the middle.

"Cards." I laugh. "You gamble your mortal soul with cards."

"I have chosen the weapons of our duel. I trust you will find I am more than skilled with these particular implements."

"And you will find I have wagered for centuries with men who live and die by the turn of a card. All of them are long dead and buried and still I remain."

"So, you agree to this contest?"

Something about this smells wrong, but even armed with the Janus dagger, this child has no hope of besting me. "I agree."

"All right." She flips the three cards over. "There are three cards. The first is the king of hearts. That card represents you and the thirteen hearts you hold in your grasp."

I allow my glaze to pass across her left breast and lick my lips. "You mean fourteen."

She attempts to hide a shudder as she points to the second card. "The queen of spades represents me and my interests."

"And the jack of diamonds?"

"The jack represents chance."

It seems inconceivable that this woman dares to come before me with no more than a six-century-old con. A part of me remembers the old adage about betting against the house, but in most gambling halls, one cannot simply flay the dealer with your bare hands if dissatisfied with a particular deal.

"Very well." I rest my elbows on the table. "What is your game?"

She takes a deep breath. "I will perform up to thirteen shuffles of these three cards, one for each of the children upstairs. After each, you will choose which you believe to be the king. If you choose correctly, a point goes to you, but if you choose incorrectly a point goes either to me or to chance. Defeat me, and my life and soul are forfeit. If in the end, however, you choose the queen more than the king, the children and I walk. No fuss, no muss."

"And if by some miracle, chance ends up with the most points?"

Her hand goes to the hilt of her weapon. "Then all bets are off. Agreed?"

"Agreed." I chuckle, knowing full well my vision can pick out the flick of a gnat's wings at a thousand yards in the dead of night. "Know that you are a fool."

"That remains to be seen." She shuffles the cards on the table. No doubt she thinks the conversation has distracted me from which card is the king. She's wrong.

"The one on the left." She flips the card and the king's eyes stare up at both of us. A flash of fear crosses her features. "A point for me."

She inhales sharply. "This contest is far from over." She flips the card back over and shuffles again. "Though you indeed are sharp of eye, Lord Solomon."

"You have no idea." When she stops shuffling, I gesture to the card in the center. "There, in the middle." She flips the card. Again, the king of hearts stands revealed and for the second time, I feel her fear. Cold and rich, like a decadent dessert, it stokes my hunger for the main course.

I gesture to the cards. "Again."

After a moment's hesitation, she begins to shuffle the cards for a third run and works them this time for over a minute.

"Frightened, necromancer?"

"I play for my soul, Lord Solomon. Pardon me if I choose to be thorough." She completes the shuffle and rests her hands in her lap.

I stare down at the cards. "Your shuffle was not thorough enough, woman. The king rests there in the center again." Her gaze flicks up to mine before it returns to the table. She rests her hand on the middle card, then flips it over. For the third time running, the king of hearts.

"Poor girl. Your efforts are noble, but I was stealing souls with this game before your ancestors crossed the Atlantic on their leaky boats."

"You haven't won yet." Though her tone reeks of bravado, a bead of sweat works its way down her brow and heads for her nose. The stress is clearly getting the best of her. She shuffles the cards again, this time as quickly as possible.

I chuckle. "Are you always so unprepared when you play games with your life?"

"I'm still alive, aren't I?" She tries to keep the tremor from her voice, but she may as well scream her terror at me. It's there in her darting eyes, her clammy skin, her dry lips. Yet to score a point, and I'm nearly halfway to victory by simple numbers. I'll give her this, she has courage.

I like courage.

It's so satisfying going down.

I watch her hands as she shuffles the cards, her tremulous fingers whetting my appetite with their every movement. In four more deals, either she submits or I take her by force. A big part of me hopes she resists.

"Fourth deal, Lord Solomon." She looks up at me.

"Choose."

"Clever, necromancer. You go to the center again and again, hoping I will make a different choice, but my eyes are quicker than your hands will ever be."

"That is one opinion." She passes a hand above the cards. "Choose."

"The middle one."

"The card in the center?" she asks. "You're certain?"

"Yes, you stupid cow, the one in the center." Crimson fills my vision again.

"Just making sure I understand you." Her fingers go to the middle card. She flips it over and my taunt catches in my throat.

"Queen of spades," she says. "That's one to me and three to you."

"But, that's impossible." The air fills with the scent of sulfur as my skin darkens with heat. "That card is the king."

She flips over the card to her right. "You mean this card?"

The table buckles and chars in my grasp. "An anomaly. Prepare your cards again."

She flips the two cards face down and shuffles anew.

"As I understand it, the men who summoned you here used the blood of those thirteen children in the original ceremony." One of her eyebrows raises as she glances up at me. "If the children are freed, there's nothing keeping you here, am I correct?"

"Lay down your cards." Her hands moved more slowly this time, more deliberately. Easy to follow, the king is clearly in the center, but it was clearly in the center on her last deal. Something is amiss.

"As you wish, Lord Solomon." Her mouth turns up in an infuriating grin. "Choose."

I start to reach for the middle card, but at the last second, gesture to the one to her left. "There, on the right. You put the king there."

"I'm so sorry, but you should have gone with your first instinct." Her shoulders slump in mock disappointment. "Your card is here in the center." She flips over the king. "See?"

"What card is that, then?" I feel my skin begin to boil. "Show me the card."

She flips it over. Flames erupt inside my chest.

"It seems you've picked the jack of diamonds."

The section of table in my grasp crumbles into chunks of ash. "It seems I have."

I am silent as she begins to shuffle again. It is clear that I am being deceived, but I know every trick, every ploy, every sleight of hand. How a mortal girl with less than three decades on this planet can achieve such seamless legerdemain is beyond my understanding.

And yet, she's done it twice in a row.

She places the three cards before me. I've tracked the king from the moment she flipped it face down. The king rests to her right. There's not a doubt in my mind.

And yet there is.

Damn her.

Damn her to Hell.

"The left. That one."

Again, with that maddening grin. "So sorry." She flips it over. Queen of spades.

"Damn you." Wisps of smoke erupt from my mouth as I exhale. "What trickery is this?"

"Just a simple game of Three-Card Monte. You proved most observant in the beginning, but it would seem you've grown fatigued as the game has progressed."

"Fatigued?" Out of my chair before I can stop myself, I pound a smoking fist upon the table. "I am immortal, you short-lived hunk of flesh. I walked this earth before your species even became upright. Something has indeed changed, but it is not me."

Her head turns to one side, her eyebrows raised and grin firmly in place. "You agreed to this game and to its rules. Am I to understand you no longer wish to play? Forfeit and let me leave with the children and the game is over. However, if you remain confident in your abilities…"

I pull in the fire and sit back down. "Put the damn cards on the table."

She flips all three cards so I can see them. "Just so you know I haven't exchanged any of the cards, here they are just as before. In fact…" She takes each card and puts them to her lips, leaving a kiss on each of the royal faces. "Now, they're marked. Satisfactory?"

"Just flip the cards and play your game."

Three times hence I watch her shuffle, and each time I'm certain my eyes don't leave the king, and yet in the next three turns, I pick the jack twice and the queen once.

"That's three apiece, my lord. Would you play again?"

I lean back in the chair, its metal creaking beneath the weight and heat of my body as a different idea occurs to me. "Indeed. Another hand, if you please."

As she flips the cards, I change tactics and follow the queen rather than the king. Somehow she is replacing the card I am watching with the one of her choice. But if I, in turn, watch the wrong one, perhaps her house of cards will fall.

"There." I point to the card on the left. "That one."

She freezes for a moment. "This one?"

A brimstone snort escapes my flaring nostrils. "I may

bellow hellfire when my temper is piqued, but I do not stutter. Show me the card."

She flips it over. There, bearing the mark of her blood red lipstick, the king of hearts stares up at the both of us.

"That's four to me, necromancer." I smile even as that damned grin evaporates from her face. "Would you play again?"

Her eyes grow wide as her own words echo back at her. Slowly, she picks up the three cards, places them between us, then flips them over and begins to shuffle again. I watch the jack this time, quite certain she will go there next.

"That one."

"The one in the middle?"

"Quit repeating what I say." Again, I pull back on the fire raging in my chest. "Yes. The one in the middle."

Her eyes narrow as she reaches for the card. "Your choice."

She flips it over, the flash of red bringing a snarling smile to my face until I lock eyes on the face staring up at me.

Jack of diamonds.

"But, how?"

"You watch my hands, my lord. I watch your eyes. You followed the jack through the entire last shuffle. What did you expect to find when I stopped?"

A low growl builds deep in my chest, the inferno of my true form begging for release.

"Lord Solomon, I understand your frustration. There are but two hands remaining. Forfeit and this is over."

"In two hands, you will be no more than a light repast before dinner. Now, lay the damned cards on the table."

Taking special care to show me each of the cards, she lays each face down and begins her careful shuffling again. I bring every iota of concentration to bear against her. The girl's crooked smirk acts as a bellows to the heat at my core.

"Twelfth hand, Lord Solomon," she says as she finishes manipulating the cards. "Choose."

Instinctively, I reach for the card on the left, but pull my hand back and hold my tongue. She has watched me and gained an advantage. Perhaps if I watch her.

Her hand trembling, her eyes look anywhere but at the card by her left thumb. Beads of sweat course down her face. She knows she has revealed the king and for a third time her fear washes across me like a refreshing breeze at the gates of Hell.

"It's that one." My hand almost shakes with excitement. "The one on your left."

Her face blanches. "Are you certain that's the card you want?"

"No more stalling. Turn over the card and let us finish this."

"And I would finish this if I could, but I'm afraid that's impossible."

"What?"

"It seems there is one more hand to play."

She flips over the card to her left.

The one I picked.

Queen of spades.

"Why you deceitful little—"

"Now, now, Lord Solomon. You know what they say about pots and kettles. When I've wracked up a few centuries of tricking people out of their immortal souls, we'll talk. Right now, you've agreed to a game, and however much it pains you, you are going to see it through. The points stand at four to you, four to me, and four to chance. One last hand to decide it all?"

I hold for a moment, running every conceivable scenario through my mind.

"Very well."

Her hands alternate between confident and tremulous as she gathers up the three folded cards and starts the thirteenth and final round of our little game. She shuffles for a long while, first slowly and deliberately, then as quickly as her nimble fingers will allow. She finishes, but as she pulls her hands away, one of her fingers flips the middle card, revealing the jack.

"Please, allow me to start again."

"You've shuffled quite enough this evening. And how appropriate that it's come down to this. Two cards. Two fates."

Striving to keep the fear from her voice, she leans in, her wicked grin a bit tarnished in the heat of the moment. "Two fates, indeed, but which will you choose?"

The two cards rest face down by either of her hands, while the jack of diamonds lays askew between them.

Chance. As if she has one. If I choose the king, I feast upon her soul and if I choose the queen I feast upon her heart.

A wise man once taught me that if you make it impossible to lose, then you will always win. For such invaluable wisdom, I did as I said I would and ate him quickly.

"That one."

She pauses, staring at the card by her right hand. "This card?"

I remove any hint of anger or frustration from my voice and offer the girl a genteel wave. "Show me the card."

Her fingers tremble as she reaches for her fate.

"Well played, my lord. Well played. This game and our battle of wits, however, belongs to chance."

I bristle at her hesitation. "What do you mean?"

"It's always been chance, from the beginning of our so-called battle of wits. The chance that I'd arrive in time, that you'd take the time to speak and not just rip out my throat, that your pride would convince you to play a game of cards, even when you probably guessed the deck was stacked against you." She flips the card, resting it on the jack of diamonds at the table's center. Impossible as it seems, this card is the jack of diamonds as well.

"What?" The skin of my face begins to smoke, obscuring my vision for a moment.

She flips the third card. A third jack of diamonds. All three bear the mark of her kiss.

My human shell begins to melt as I launch out of my chair. "Enough of your games, necromancer. Tonight, you die."

"You'd best hurry, then. Your time, as you can see, is limited." She gestures past me at the bank of monitors. I glance across my shoulder at the screen where before the children lay bound and gagged around my summoning circle. The children are gone, replaced by the two dozen or so men in my employ, not to mention the sorcerer priest who brought me here in the first place. To the man, they are cuffed and under guard of what passes for constables in this land.

"A distraction. That's all you were. A pretty distraction."

She pulls the Janus dagger from its sheath. "Any last words?"

I laugh, my breath coming out like blue flame. "Even without the children, I have until sunrise. More than enough time for a light snack." In a blink, I grab the heavy metal table and fling it at her, only to gasp as it passes right through her.

A pain like a coal from the deepest pits fills my back. I look down to find the tip of the Janus dagger protruding from my chest.

"Go back to Hell," comes Sullivan's voice from behind me, suddenly clearer than I've heard since she first revealed herself. A simple thought crosses my mind. I first noticed the glamour coming off the amulet mere seconds after I watched her walk across the screen. I suppose she truly was putting on a show.

"Oh," she adds, "Bindlekroff sends his regards."

I fall to my knees, the silver radiance of the Elder Blade spilling out around and through me. "Bindlekroff?"

"He asked me to remind you of the lesson he taught you many years ago, that there is power in illusion, but more importantly, that power *is* an illusion."

"He sent you. That rat bastard."

"You ate his daughter," she rumbles, "you demonic piece of shit."

My human form nearly shed, I stand revealed, my blackened skin even now disintegrating into nothingness as the Janus dagger works at my already tenuous hold on this plane. I try to speak, but my voice has abandoned me.

"Let me tell you something that crossed my mind today. I've heard hundreds of legends, read all the books, seen all the movies. Most every story since the dawn of man has a villain, a bogeyman, a big bad that comes for the hero in the end." She pulls her sarcastic angel's face around close to where I can just see her out of the corner of my eye. "Understand that you've just met yours."

As my hold on reality begins to fade, a thought occurs to me. I summon whatever will I have remaining and push a single word from my lips.

"Question."

"What?" she asks.

"You wagered your life, the lives of the children, your very soul for a single answer. What was the question?"

She twists the blade in my back and pulls my body to the floor. As the hilt strikes the concrete, the dagger drives deeper into my fiery core. The lancinating pain in my chest flares even as all sensation abandons my quickly disintegrating corporeal form.

"We've been talking for an hour," she says, "and yet there is one word I long to hear straight from your lips."

She pulls in tight and whispers three simple syllables into what remains of my blackened ear.

"What's my name?"

# Symphony of Wolves

April's body tensed from scalp to sole as lights flickered throughout the atrium. Her pulse quickening, she scanned the crowd. Men in suits and women in dresses that cost more than she made in half a year surrounded her, all unaware of the danger about to reveal itself. Gavin caught her hand as it went for the latch of her purse.

"It's just intermission ending, April. No need for Georgetown's resident necromancer to start flashing steel." Gavin lowered his voice as a devilish grin spread across his face. "Unless you suspect a horde of zombies is about to pour out of that coat closet over there."

April squeezed his hand for a moment, then relaxed her grip. "Sorry. Hard to turn it off sometimes. First night of the full moon always leaves me a little antsy."

"This should help." Gavin paid the bartender and handed April a glass of champagne. "And don't feel bad. My first year out of the academy, I jumped every time a car backfired. In both our lines of work, our instincts are what keep us alive." He pulled her close and whispered in her ear. "Not to mention, the things I chase through the night can't turn around and eat me."

April smiled and took a sip of the bubbly, then put it

down as a wave of nausea coursed through her body. Giving the room a second visual sweep, she asked, "So, anything to all that full moon stuff you hear about in the funny papers? Things that go bump in the night aside, of course. Violent crimes? ER visits? 911 calls?"

"We had a lecture on urban legends back at the academy. Seems all the years of research on the topic have never shown any measurable effect of the moon on human behavior," Gavin raised an eyebrow. "Talk to any guy on the force who's been around a while, though, and you'll get a different story."

April crossed her arms and rubbed at the goosebumps overlying her triceps. The air in the atrium a bit chilly for her taste, she wished she hadn't left her wrap at their seats. "So what do you think of the show so far?"

"Not my usual speed, but it's not bad considering the last concert you took me to left me half deaf for a couple days."

"I don't remember dragging you to see Metallica. In fact, as I recall, it was all but your idea." April shot him a wicked smile. "And I did offer you earplugs."

Gavin puffed up his chest. "Real men don't wear earplugs."

"Neither do deaf people."

Gavin pulled her close, his dark suit flavoring the air with just a hint of cologne. "You wound me, fair lady."

"Just saying, we were close enough to count the beads of sweat on Kirk Hammett's forehead." April brought the champagne to her lips again, and the tightening in the pit of her stomach returned. She handed the glass to Gavin who took a gulp and set it back on the bar.

"If the show so far is any indication, we won't be needing any earplugs tonight, unless the orchestra really rocks it out during the second half."

April swatted his arm. "Make fun all you want. I saw that foot of yours tapping before."

"What can I say?" Gavin shrugged. "I've got on my dancing shoes tonight."

"Oh, don't you worry. There's going to be dancing later." April stepped away from him and swept her shoulders back, accentuating the form-fitting blue dress and knee-high boots she had put together for the evening. "I'd hate for all this effort to go to waste."

"Nothing to worry about there." Gavin grinned. "The guy sitting next to you in our box definitely appreciates your efforts this evening."

April chuckled. "His poor wife. I don't think he said a word to her the whole first half."

"And box seats sounded like such a great idea."

"I have to say…" April bit her lip. "It was kind of cute when you wrapped your coat around me."

Gavin let out a quiet hmmph. "You looked cold."

"And I thought you did it because I looked hot." The lights flickered again. April grabbed Gavin's hand and gave it a squeeze, a promise for later. "We'd better get back."

Their box seats overlooked the right half of the stage, the home of the brass section. Gavin traded seats with April, putting some distance between her and her erstwhile admirer. As the lights flickered one last time, Gavin pulled out his program.

"I hope the second half has a little more meat to it. That last piece didn't really kick in till the end."

"Stravinsky's *Firebird* is a little, well, flighty at times. The second half, though, starts with the Mussorgsky piece. You know *Night on Bald Mountain*, right?"

Gavin stroked his chin. "Sounds… familiar."

"It was in *Fantasia*, the part at the end with Chernobog."

At Gavin's blank stare, she added, "The big demon on the mountain."

"After last month, I'd think you'd be done with big demons."

A shiver ran up April's spine. "Just trust me. You know this one."

Applause filled the hall as the conductor took the stage, his every step paced by a brilliant spotlight. Stepping to the podium, he turned to face the crowd and the room fell silent. April flashed on a favorite cartoon from Saturday morning an eternity before.

"Hey," April whispered in Gavin's ear. "What was it the orchestra called Bugs Bunny when he was conducting the big fat opera singer?"

Without missing a beat, Gavin answered, "Leopold."

"That's it." April checked her program. "So, how do you think this Harrison Rafe guy rates against my favorite 'wascally wabbit' in wig and tails?"

"I guess we'll see." Gavin rested a hand on April's knee as the conductor began to speak.

Rafe spent a couple minutes introducing the next piece, his British accent so crisp that April would have listened to him read the phone book. When he was done, he turned to face the orchestra. At his subtle wave, the violins began with the warbling sound that had made April's hair stand on end since she was a little girl. The woodwinds and brass soon followed suit, and a song that had haunted her imagination for years filled the air. As the soundtrack of her nightmares approached the halfway point, the main melody came back around, and April took Gavin's hand in the dark. He squeezed hers back, his grip firm yet gentle, and for just a moment, the evening was perfect.

That was when the screaming started.

April's gaze shot down onto the stage as the orchestra fell silent. The lead violinist, an alluring woman with long flowing black hair and dark eyes fell to the floor, her arms and legs convulsing as if she were being electrocuted.

*Or possessed.* April rubbed at her brow. *God, I've got to take a vacation.*

"What do you think?" Gavin whispered in her ear. "Seizure?"

The well-coiffed woman to their left whispered to her husband. "Get down there, honey. That girl needs your help." As the man exited the box, the woman turned to April and Gavin. "That's Rebecca Bouchard, the French violinist. She's on loan to us this season from the Orchestre de Paris." She glanced in the direction her husband had gone. "My David is a neurologist. If anyone can help her, he can."

April's lips grew tight as she watched at the events unfolding below. "No offense to your husband, ma'am, but I don't think anyone is going to be able to help Ms. Bouchard tonight."

Gavin and the woman followed her stare and the three of them watched in horror as jet-black hair sprouted from every inch of the beautiful violinist's skin. Her body contorted, changing shape as if some invisible sculptor were reshaping her bones and sinew. Fingers stretched and curled into fur-covered claws, ears lengthened and moved atop her head, while mouth and nose elongated into a snout filled with glistening, razor-sharp teeth.

April pulled the woman to her. "Go find your husband and get the hell out of here."

The woman raced from the box, leaving April alone with Gavin. Musicians fled the stage in all directions while the rest of the hall descended into madness as hundreds of people climbed over each other like rats fleeing a flooding sewer.

"You're packing, right?" April shouted over the screaming.

"After the thing at the funeral home?" He opened his jacket to reveal the pistol hanging at his side. "Last time I go anywhere without a gun."

"Good." April shot a glance at the stage. "Though I'm guessing you didn't bring along any silver bullets."

Gavin pulled his weapon from its holster. "You can't be serious."

"Come on, babe." April felt in her purse until her fingers found old leather wound around steel and drew the Janus dagger out into the light. "Necromancers, vampires, demons. Are werewolves really that big of a stretch?"

"I guess not." Gavin leveled his pistol at the convulsing thing on the stage that had taken the place of the beautiful violinist. "Any tips?"

"I don't know." April looked away. "I've never run into a werewolf before."

"Seriously?"

"Nope." April glanced back at Gavin. "This is a first."

"Wow." Gavin ran a sleeve across his brow. "There's something you haven't seen. Not sure if I'm relieved or scared shitless."

"Not to say I haven't picked up a few tidbits over the years. Werewolves are strong, fast, vicious killers. Silver works as billed, but as I understand it, the wound has to be lethal. Same for weapons with a glimmer of magic. As for guns, though, a warlock I used to deal with told me he saw one of these things take a twelve-gauge shot to the muzzle. Didn't even slow it down."

Gavin sighed as he gestured to the glowing weapon in

April's not quite trembling hand. "Sounds like your dagger there is the best thing we've got going, then."

"Mystic blades for mystic beasts." April gripped the hilt even more tightly as a blood-curdling howl echoed in the acoustically perfect room. "I guess we'll find out."

The creature that had been Rebecca Bouchard rose onto its hind legs. Its muscular form freed from the woman's modest black dress, the wolf threw its head back, and sniffed the air before resuming its awful baying. April surveyed the room. Save for the many trampled and the few morbidly curious enough to try to document the event with their cameras and phones, the vast hall had emptied. Most of the doorways, however, remained clogged with people scrambling over each other trying to escape. The orchestra players had fled to the wings, other than a select few who remained, apparently too frightened to move.

"Dozens of people everywhere and unless I miss my guess, that thing is hungry." April ground her teeth. "There's going to be a bloodbath."

Suddenly silent other than for its coarse breathing, the wolf glared around the room, then without warning, bounded off the stage and into the wing below April and Gavin's box.

Before April could say it, Gavin said exactly what was on her mind. "I'm not sure, but it seems like she – it – is looking for something."

"Or someone." April peered over the side of the box. "We've got to get down there."

Gavin glanced toward the door. "We'll never be able to push past the crowd if we take the stairs."

"Then I guess we do it the hard way." April gestured to the three-story cloth banner stretching from ceiling to floor next to their box.

"You've seen one too many Jackie Chan movies."

"Hey. It's the shortest distance between two points." April whipped the banner into a cord and stepped to the edge of the box. "You coming?" Wishing she were in her favorite pair of jeans, April hitched up her dress, wrapped her ankles around the twisted banner, and slid down the makeshift rope. Once her feet reached the floor below, she shouted for Gavin to follow. Barely halfway down, the banner tore under his weight and Gavin landed in a pile on the unforgiving floor.

April rushed to his side. "Are you all right?"

Gavin grabbed one of the seats to his left and winced as he pulled himself to his feet. "I've had worse." A rueful smile spread across his face. "Though my thigh would like to remind everyone that it took a bullet a couple months back." Gavin climbed onto the stage and headed for the wings, a subtle limp the only sign that he was injured. "You coming?"

"Smart ass," April muttered as she followed Gavin's lead.

Once on stage, April directed the few remaining musicians to head for the exits at the back of the auditorium, then joined Gavin at the double door leading backstage.

"On three?" At Gavin's nod, she turned the dagger pommel up in her hand the way her teacher, Julian, had taught her and uttered, "Three." They burst through the door together and took positions at each other's six. Rather than the scene out of a Tarantino flick April expected, they found only one body, and no blood. She rushed to the downed man's side and felt his neck. Though fast and weak, he still had a pulse and appeared for the most part uninjured.

"He's alive." April looked back. "Weird. I figured we'd be following a trail of bodies."

Another howl echoed through the backstage area.

Gavin charged past her. "Guess we'll have to follow the howling instead."

They circled around behind the stage area, coming upon musician after musician hidden in every nook and cranny of the place. Miraculously, the wolf had left them all alive.

"A werewolf is a killing machine," April said.

Gavin turned to her, a puzzled look across his features. "So, why isn't anyone dead?"

A new sound filled the air, the sound of splintering wood. Gavin and April raced around the next corner to find the wolf ramming its shoulder again and again into a closed double door. Though humanoid in posture, the thing seemed to have forgotten how to use its hands as anything other than bludgeons. Between blows, April could just make out the sound of screams from the other side.

"It's got someone trapped in that closet," Gavin said.

"Hey, ugly," April shouted. "Get away from there."

The wolf turned on her and Gavin, its chest pumping like a bellows. Eight feet high and as wide as April's VW Beetle, it leered at them, though it made no move to engage them in any way. Instead, it studied them for a moment, then turned and slashed at the door, carving a set of four parallel gouges in the wood. Another scream filtered through the shredded doors.

A woman's scream.

April held the shimmering Janus dagger before her and advanced on the wolf. As silver and magic were the order of the day, she took comfort in the fact that this particular Elder Blade comprised plenty of both. As she drew close, the wolf backed away, much like a vampire retreating from a crucifix, and yet different somehow. This withdrawal seemed less about repulsion and more about respect.

"That's right," April said. "Back away from the door like a good puppy."

To April's left, Gavin leveled his pistol at the wolf. "If

that thing so much as breathes funny…"

"You'll what? Piss it off?" April asked. "Remember, no silver, no dice."

Gavin cracked his neck. "You'd rather I just attack the thing with my bare hands?"

"Sorry, babe. It's just I'd prefer if you stayed in one piece."

April and Gavin continued their slow advance, backing the wolf further and further toward the corner of the room. April flashed on a childhood memory of her father warning her about cornering a wild animal, but at the moment, she didn't see that she had much choice.

"Gavin," she said, "I've got this. Get whoever that is in the closet to safety."

"And what are you planning to do?"

April crinkled her nose. "Keep tall, dark, and ugly here at bay."

Never once taking her eyes off the mountain of fur, muscle, and sinew before her, April listened as Gavin coaxed the woman into letting him help her. At the sound of the turning latch, the wolf before her hunched as if to jump.

"Now, now." April held the Janus dagger in one hand, her other hand held out before her palm out like a traffic cop. "Stay, Fido."

The wolf made no gesture of recognition beyond narrowing its dark eyes, though April was confident the woman within the wolf understood her every word.

April chanced a glance back as Gavin coaxed the woman from the closet. Dressed in a revealing white sequined dress, the exquisite beauty stepped through the battered doorway, her flashing blue eyes filled with trepidation. Bright blond hair flowed in ringlets past her shoulders. April remembered reading about the world-renowned singer in the program. Alessandra Ducat, her elfin features as beautiful as her well-trained voice, was to have been the lead soprano for the final piece of the evening, Mozart's *Requiem*.

No sooner was Ducat free from her self-imposed prison than the wolf roared and dove past April, its form a dark blur of fur, tooth, and claw.

"Incoming!" April lashed out with the Janus dagger as the wolf passed her, but if the enchanted blade so much as scratched its hide, the wolf gave no indication. Gavin spun and fired two rounds into the thing's belly before it was upon them and a fur-covered backhanded blow sent him sprawling into the far wall.

"Gavin!" April ran at them, but stopped short when the wolf's hand shot out and seized the woman by her long blond locks. Her every instinct screamed to run to her lover's side, but she kept control and focused on the task at hand: keeping the pretty soprano's insides inside her.

Her toes dangling two feet above the floor, Ducat hung helpless from the beast's outstretched arm, her piercing blue eyes filled with terror. Still, the wolf didn't strike.

"What the hell are you waiting for?" April asked under her breath.

"Rebecca!" came a voice from behind April. A crisp, British voice.

April peeked across her shoulder and found Harrison Rafe approaching from the door leading to the main stage. The conductor moved with confidence, his every step sure-footed and straight. He hummed a strange melody under his breath, all the while tilting his head first to one side, then the other. The dark wolf looked on as the silver-haired conductor came closer, an expression somewhere between anger and contrition passing its lupine features.

"Rebecca, Rebecca. Come away from poor Alessandra there."

The wolf pulled the woman in white to her snout and sniffed at her midsection as if about to take a bite.

"Rebecca!" Rafe commanded. "Enough!"

The wolf glanced at the conductor once again, then released the woman. Ducat fell in a pile at the thing's feet and didn't move again.

"Now, Rebecca. To me." Despite Rafe's urging, the wolf hesitated, sniffing the air and sidling back and forth by Ducat's unconscious form. The conductor, in turn, resumed his strange humming and side-to-side head movements. A few seconds passed before the wolf left the woman, dropped onto all fours, and padded over to the man's side like a well-trained dog. Rafe stroked the jet-black fur between the wolf's ears and shot April a bone-chilling smile. Keeping one eye on the mountain of muscle and claws resting at the conductor's side and the other on the conductor himself, April ran to check on Gavin. She found him groggy, but conscious.

"You okay?" she asked.

"Not the most banged up I've been after a date with you." The forced levity in his words did little to hide the pain etched in his features. "Though I think my health insurance is going to drop me if we keep going out. And I'm union."

"Can you walk?"

"I believe so." With a little assistance, Gavin pulled himself to his feet. "Curious. Why aren't you fighting for your life?"

"I'm not quite sure." April gestured to the conductor and the eight-foot wolf lapping at his palm. "Seems Leopold here keeps a side job as a werewolf whisperer."

Gavin strode over to Rafe, the barrel of his pistol trained on the floor, and flashed his badge. "Gavin McLaren, Georgetown PD."

"My apologies, officer," Rafe said. "I had no intention of this happening."

"You didn't intend for your lead violinist to transform into a werewolf in front of hundreds of people?" April asked.

"Of course not, but that's not what I meant." Rafe knelt beside the wolf and stroked the fur along its spine. "I suppose it was only a matter of time, but I never meant this for her."

April felt the heat rise in her cheeks. "Mr. Rafe, you obviously take some satisfaction in being the only person here that knows what the hell is going on, but you must recognize that hundreds of people with photographic evidence of the existence of werewolves just took to the streets. This place is going to be swarming with cops in minutes. Invincible werewolf or not, I don't think any of us wants to watch poor Rebecca go a few rounds with Georgetown's finest."

Rafe's gaze wandered from Gavin to April to the wolf to the woman in the white dress still lying unconscious on the cold concrete. "I hate that it has come to this. Rebecca and I have been together for seven months and everything has been ideal. That is, until tonight."

Gavin's brow furrowed. "You've knowingly been seeing a werewolf."

"Says the man who came here with a mere slip of a girl who carries around one of the Elder Blades as if it were her personal nail file." He shifted his gaze toward April. "And what particular set of skills do you bring to the table, my dear?"

April sheathed the Janus dagger. "You're not the only one who holds their cards close to their chest, Mr. Rafe."

"Fair enough, Miss…?"

"Sullivan."

"Well, Miss Sullivan, how do you propose we resolve this situation?"

April glanced at the almost playful eyes of the wolf at Rafe's side. "Any chance we can get Rebecca here into a less furry state before we negotiate?"

"Unlikely on the first night of the full moon. My apologies, but I'm afraid the lovely Miss Bouchard is indisposed for the evening."

"Well, do you at least think you can keep her from pawing at your guest soprano over there?" April thumbed in the direction of the woman in white curled on the floor.

"I will do my best, Miss Sullivan, but I make no guarantees on a wolf's behavior." Rafe smiled. "It is the nature of the alpha female to show aggression toward other females in the pack."

"Especially the ones that rival them for the affections of the alpha male?" April asked.

Rafe's eyes flashed with surprise and some of the smugness evaporated from his features. "I'm afraid I don't know what you mean."

"Come on, Mr. Rafe," April said. "I may not be the local expert on werewolves, but I know a wolf when I see one."

"If only my instincts were as good as yours." The female voice came from behind April and Gavin. The wolf growled as the woman in white rose from the floor.

"Alessandra," Rafe said. "Thank God you're all right."

"Well, we certainly don't have you to thank for that, Harrison."

Rafe rose from the floor. "I assume you heard it all."

"I heard enough." She glanced at the wolf at his side. "So, this is the bitch you told me you left so you could be with me?"

The wolf came to its feet, its ears swept back and teeth bared. The growl emanating from its throat grew louder with each passing second.

"Hold your tongue, Alessandra. Provoked, Rebecca could still tear you limb from limb."

"As if I'd allow that." Alessandra's dismissive gaze passed from Rafe to Rebecca. "She is but a pup."

A quiet growl escaped Rebecca's teeth and Rafe scratched between the dark wolf's ears, doing his best to keep it – her – calm.

"You turned her." Alessandra drew her lip into a snarl. "Why?"

"Wait a minute." April glanced at Gavin, then back at Rafe. "You?"

Rafe glared at Alessandra. "Dropping secrets now, are we, my dear?"

"The Sullivan girl seems quite sharp. She would have put it together soon enough."

April took a step toward Rafe, then backed off as the wolf at his side turned its attention on her. "I don't understand. You said before you never meant this for her, and yet here we are."

Rafe rested his hand across his heart as if wounded by her words. "Do not speak to me of the curse, Miss Sullivan. I have carried this burden for longer than you can imagine." He looked down at the wolf and sighed. "Unlike poor Rebecca here, I have learned over the years to resist the monthly call of the moon. Still, I never slept with her nights when Luna was full for fear I might lose control. That is, until last month."

Alessandra's eyes narrowed in anger. "You told me you hadn't been with her since the summer, you bastard."

"I told you many things, Alessandra." Rafe turned back to April. "It was the last night of the full moon and our six month anniversary. We had just finished our last performance of Beethoven's *Ninth*. She came to my office and things got a little… heated."

"She saw you?" Alessandra said. "And yet she still stayed?"

"I didn't change, at least not outwardly." Rafe looked down with pity at Rebecca. The wolf looked back at him with an almost innocent gaze. "But in the heat of passion—"

"You bit her." April's lips drew down to tight line. "Did she know what you were and what that might mean?"

"The next morning, before she awoke, I checked her shoulder and found no wound. Not even a scratch. I assumed I hadn't broken the skin." Rafe lowered his head. "Obviously, I was wrong. We'd been together so many times over the months, it seems I allowed myself to become complacent and now, as you said, here we are."

"Yes, Harrison, here we are." Alessandra strode toward the conductor and the wolf.

"Stay back, Alessandra," Rafe said. "It doesn't have to end this way."

"Hide in the security closet," she said, drawing closer with every syllable. "Let her wear herself out. Wait for the authorities to arrive." Her lips drew wide, not so much a smile as a baring of her teeth. "I tried to play this disaster the way you asked, dear Harrison. Now we'll play it mine."

"Are you crazy?" Gavin shouted to Alessandra. "That thing was about to disembowel you a minute ago."

"Stay alert, babe." April knuckles went white as she gripped the Janus dagger. "There's more to her than meets the eye."

116

"Listen to your woman, constable." She directed a thumb in Rafe's direction. "And treat her with more respect than this dog treated me. After all, the child she carries is yours."

Gavin's eyes shot to April. "Child?"

April's free hand went instinctively to her belly. "What are you talking about?"

"You didn't know?" Alessandra sniffed the air, then shot April a lopsided grin. "Best lay off the champagne for the next few months, my dear."

"You're lying," April said, even as calendar dates ran across her mind's eye. "Whatever you're trying to pull here, it won't work."

"And what possible reason would I have to lie to you?" Alessandra asked. "Just a little advice from one woman to another." She turned to face Rafe and Rebecca. "And speaking of other women…" Alessandra released the clasp at her left shoulder and allowed her dress to fall in a white pool at her feet, her well-toned body nude beneath the elegant white gown.

April's gaze shot to Rafe, then back to Alessandra. The same self-satisfied smirk filled both their features. "Shit," she muttered.

"There can be, after all, only one alpha female in the pack." In stark contrast to Rebecca's torturous transformation, Alessandra's seemed painless and almost graceful. Bright blond hair erupted from every pore as her face drew out into a vicious muzzle punctuated on either side by those sparkling blue eyes. No sooner had Alessandra adopted her full upright posture than Rebecca was on her, a flurry of fur and teeth.

The dark wolf's jaws clamped down on the lighter wolf's haunches, and for a moment it seemed Rebecca had the upper hand. Alessandra growled and hurled herself backwards, sandwiching Rebecca between three hundred pounds of muscle and the unforgiving steel of the wall. Rebecca let out a yelp and fell dazed from Alessandra's back. Alessandra leaped upon her downed adversary and went straight for her throat.

"Stop this!" April screamed at Rafe. "She's going to kill her."

"I tried to avoid this." Rafe looked on, dispassionate. "I never meant for any of this to occur, but now that it has, the fray must take its course."

"I think you're enjoying having these two fight over you," Gavin said.

"It's not a matter of enjoyment. Within a pack, the alpha male mates with the alpha female." Rafe's gaze drifted over to the escalating brawl. "They're each just doing their best to prove their worth."

"Their worth?" April asked. "One of them has to die so the other can be with you?"

"To you, it must seem cruel, but to us, this represents nothing but centuries of well-ingrained instinct."

Alessandra straddled Rebecca, her teeth and claws opening wound after wound in the darker wolf's chest and neck. Rebecca did her best to defend herself, but April knew all too well it was only a matter of time before the blond wolf's teeth found her jugular.

Gavin limped to Rafe's side. "You're seriously going to let her kill that poor woman."

Rafe turned his emotionless gaze on Gavin. "It is simply the way of things."

"Like hell it is." Gavin raised his pistol and aimed at the blond wolf, but before he could pull the trigger, a flash of white sent the gun flying from his hand.

Where Rafe had stood moments before now stood a white wolf-thing reared up on its hind legs. The conductor's dark tuxedo in tatters, the pelt beneath shone as blinding as an arctic snow. Even hunched, the Rafe-wolf stood two feet taller than Gavin. Thick drool ran from its bared teeth as it let out a low growl.

"Gavin," April shouted. "Don't move."

Gavin stood frozen to the spot. The white wolf leaned into Gavin's space, sniffing the air around his neck. April felt her toes curl in her boots as the fear at her core blossomed into anger.

"Get away from him!" Her command ignored, April shouted again. "I said, get away from him, you bastard!" Her anger and fear escalating into white-hot rage, April felt a sudden calm fall upon her. "Fine," she whispered. "Two can play at that game."

April ran at the pair of female wolves and plunged the Janus dagger into the blond wolf's shoulder. The blade glowed silver and the Alessandra-wolf yelped in surprise and agony before falling to one side, leaving the wounded Rebecca-wolf gasping for air.

The white wolf spun and raced at April as if Gavin were no more than a distant memory. Rafe was on her in a second, an ivory whirlwind of fur and fangs. Its pearl claws left four parallel trails of blood on her arm as it swatted the blade from her hand. The Janus dagger flew across the room and stuck in the wall, the Elder Blade piercing the thick steel like an icepick through tin foil.

If the white wolf towered over Gavin, it eclipsed April. Something like a smile floated across its lupine features as it advanced on her, almost as if it could smell the fear mounting in her chest. With each step backward, April knew the wall was drawing closer and she would have nowhere else to run. As her hand found the bolts protruding from the steel wall behind her, she closed her eyes and awaited the inevitable.

*Play with fire long enough…*

The white wolf bellowed in rage and pain as the dark wolf sank its teeth into the side of its neck. April ducked under its flailing claws and ran to the far wall where Gavin was madly pulling at the Janus dagger. Even together, they couldn't free the blade from its steely prison.

"I found my gun," Gavin said, "not that it's going to do much good."

"Yeah," April said. "Bullets would probably just make them madder."

The pair of wolves, one white, one black, both covered in wet crimson, went at each other with a ferocity April had never witnessed.

Gavin's expression grew distant. "Is it true?"

"Not now, babe. Not now." April slung Gavin's arm across her shoulder and as fast as they could move, headed back to the main hall. Without missing a step, April kicked the double door closed behind them and shoved a chair leg through the door handles before continuing their dash for the exit.

"Don't look now," Gavin said as they reached the center of the stage, "but we might just make it out of this alive."

No sooner had Gavin spoken the words than the door behind them exploded into a million fragments of wood and steel. The white wolf, its muzzle smeared with vermilion gore stood in the doorway panting. Though wounded, the Rafe-wolf still looked more than capable of ending them both with no more effort than swatting a fly. With enraged eyes, it scanned the stage until its gaze settled on April.

April shoved Gavin toward the stairs and turned to face Rafe, panic gripping her heart as the wolf crouched to leap. Weaponless and terrified, she cast about for anything that might give her a fighting chance.

And there they were. Behind the abandoned string section.

In the moment between breaths, a voice from the past echoed through April's mind.

"You stupid, brainless idiot."

Ninth grade band, the last five minutes before Christmas break, and the bell couldn't ring soon enough for April. Rushing to the storage room to put away her instrument, she heard someone call her name and spun around on one heel. That's when it happened.

Her horn clanged off the flute of the girl behind her.

And it wasn't just any girl.

It was Kitty Snellenger. Self proclaimed queen of the class, and April's sworn nemesis.

"Sorry. Didn't mean to hit your flute." April bit her lip. "But hey, at least it's a loaner."

"A loaner? I'll have you know, April Sullivan, that this was my mother's flute." She inclined her head to one side and crinkled her nose. "Like I'd play an instrument that's been blown on by God knows how many before me."

"I said I was sorry."

Kitty inspected her instrument. "Great. Now there's a ding in it. Do you have any idea how much a flute like this costs?" Her lips spread into a conceited smile. "Mother's flute is professional grade, and professionals insist on…"

"Silver." April ducked beneath the white wolf's slashing claws and ran for the woodwind section. The pair of flutes lay discarded by an overturned chair. Diving at the floor, she grabbed one in each hand, went into the first cartwheel she'd performed since junior high, and rounded off to land facing the wolf.

"All right, Mr. Big Bad Wolf," she said. "Here I am."

The wolf's lips pulled back from its teeth in an angry snarl, but its eyes were glued to the pair of solid silver singlesticks in its adversary's hands. A low growl issued from its throat, and April's knees knocked despite her best efforts to keep them still.

"Stay away from her, you animal!" Gavin backed up his words with two rounds from his pistol. The white wolf spun, its low growl reaching a fever pitch.

"Gavin!" April screamed. "No!"

Rafe leaped at Gavin, a blur of ivory and crimson. Gavin got off one last shot before the beast was on him. April ran at them, her twin weapons glinting in the stage lights, her only shot at saving Gavin from a painful, bloody death. Or a fate far, far worse.

April came at Rafe from behind and pulled the flutes back, forming a flashing silver X above her head, then brought them down on either side of the wolf's head, boxing its ears. The thing howled, its front paw slashing out and ripping the front of April's dress. The four parallel lines that crossed April's abdomen seeped scarlet. Less than an inch from being eviscerated, she fought past the pain and stabbed at the wolf, its head turned to the side to see the damage it had wrought. With every ounce of her strength, she buried the tube of solid silver in the wolf's left eye socket, the sickening wet sound followed by a cry that would have made the wailing in Hell stop their screaming for a moment and listen.

Throwing itself from Gavin's unmoving form, the wolf leaped from the stage with the two feet of metal still protruding from its skull. Turning to glare at April, it reached up with one blood-covered paw, wrenched the flute from its eye and hurled it into the far corner of the auditorium.

"Sullivan," it hissed. The only word any of the wolves had spoken, it chilled April to the core. She took a step forward and held the remaining flute before her.

"You want some more, Rafe, then come and get me, motherfucker."

The white wolf glared at her for another moment, then sprinted for the rear of the auditorium, hitting one of the doors like an ivory-furred battering ram before disappearing into the foyer beyond.

The flute dropped from April's trembling fingers as she ran to Gavin's side and knelt beside his still form, her heart hammering in her chest.

"Gavin?" she whispered. "Can you hear me?"

She felt at his neck and found his pulse quick but surprisingly strong. Blood covered his shirt and chest, but none of it appeared to be his. Icy guilt gripped her heart as she considered how many times in their short relationship she'd been forced to see him in pain.

"I swear sometimes, Gavin," she muttered. "You'd be better off if we'd never met."

"And miss all the fun?" His whisper was so quiet, April could barely make out the words.

"Thank God." April gently hugged his neck. "Are you all right?"

"I'll tell you in a minute." His eyes half-opened and glanced to the left. "Is Rafe gone?"

"He bolted." The door at the rear of the auditorium still hanging from one hinge, April half expected the wolf to reappear at any moment to finish the job. The image of his one bloody eye socket flashed across her memory. "Though I have a sinking suspicion he won't be forgetting me anytime soon."

Gavin tried to sit up, but barely made it up onto one elbow. April helped him to his feet, and the two of them limped together to the backstage area. Where the dark wolf's mutilated body had been, Rebecca Bouchard's body lay unmoving and pale in a pool of quickly congealing blood. Other than a few tufts of blond fur, however, the wolf that was Alessandra Ducat had disappeared.

"Fantastic," April muttered. "Both of them."

April and Gavin made their way over to the Janus dagger, still imbedded in the steel wall. Between the two of them and a long metal curtain rod that functioned as a makeshift lever, they were able to pry the blade loose. April had just returned the weapon to her purse when a bustle of activity started at the large double door leading to the loading dock.

"Nobody move!" A uniformed officer shouted as police swarmed the room. "Hands in the air, you two!"

"Don't shoot." Gavin flashed the badge on his belt. "Georgetown PD."

The officer glanced at April's belly. "You're bleeding pretty badly. I'll get help." The cop looked across his shoulder. "Medic!"

Unable to speak, April stared down at the four parallel slashes across her abdomen and wondered if what Ducat had said could possibly be true.

"Is it possible?" she whispered to herself. "A baby?"

Two pairs of paramedics rushed into the room with stretchers and aid bags. One pair went to check on Rebecca, the other to Gavin and April.

"What happened here?" the first paramedic asked. "We got a call about a wild animal loose in the auditorium."

Before either of them could answer, the other paramedic glanced down at Gavin's arm. "Hey. You're bleeding too."

April's gaze trained on Gavin's forearm like a laser. From beneath the jacket draped across his arm, fresh blood dripped from his fingers and onto the hardwood floor at their feet. Before

Gavin could stop her, April pulled the jacket from his arm. Just above his wrist was a crescent-shaped wound far too jagged and far too curved to have come from the wolf's claws.

"How did I miss that?" April locked gazes with Gavin. "Wait. You hid this from me?"

Gavin glanced at her navel. "Like I'm the only one hiding things tonight."

April sighed. "You really want to do this now?"

"No." Gavin held out his arm and allowed the paramedic to get to work. "I guess not."

Neither of them said a word as the paramedics bandaged their wounds, loaded them into the ambulance, and started an IV line in each of their arms.

"You two are real lucky. Whatever that thing was that tore into you looks like it was hell on wheels, but neither of your wounds look too bad." A yell from outside got the paramedic's attention. "Excuse me a minute."

Alone for the first time since the cops arrived, April found a spare blanket and put it around Gavin's shaking form. In their few months together, she'd never seen him cry. She didn't say a word, but kept him close by her side.

"I was only a few days late." April stroked Gavin's neck. "I didn't want to worry you. Hell, I didn't want to worry me."

"Well, we're headed to the hospital, so I guess we'll know soon enough."

April glanced at the bandage on Gavin's wrist. "At least on my end."

"So, what now?" Gavin whispered.

"Rafe and Ducat are still on the loose, and they know my name and both of our scents." April closed her eyes and took a deep breath through her nose. "I can't imagine they're not going to come for us, so we'd best prepare."

"That's not what I'm talking about," Gavin said.

"I know." April looked through the rear window of the ambulance at the full moon, its pale light filling the sky just above the row of buildings across the street. "A lot of things will be clearer in the morning, but for now, I'd say we've both got a long month ahead of us."

# THE FALL AND RISE OF JULIAN LAMORTE

Damn her.

Damn the witch to this very hell to which she has condemned me these last months: an intangible wraith, invisible to the world, unwilling voyeur to every last moment of her banal existence, unable to escape her presence for even a moment. Oh, for one last chance to grapple with Sullivan face to face, this student to whom I entrusted everything. I'd carve that smug smile from her ripe mouth and remind her which of us is the master.

But no. My lot now is to observe in silence. And hers? To live. To experience. To breathe.

If that were all, if she had but picked up where I left off and simply walked the path of the necromancer to its inexorable end, my fate would be at least tolerable, but even that cold comfort is denied me. For it would seem that April Sullivan, my once apprentice, has allowed herself to fall in love. And so content is she with her newfound love, she has forgotten who she is.

What she is.

That, more than anything, is the thought that fills my every mute moment with silent fury.

"Everything dies," I taught her our first day together as student and teacher, a lesson I myself learned what now seems an eternity ago. "The only common denominator between the highest form of life on this planet and the lowest, man and microbe alike, is that in the end, Death awaits us all."

"But Death isn't the end," she said. "That's what you told me when we first met."

"A matter of perspective. Death, you see, is both an ending and a beginning." I remember actually smiling in that moment, unaware of the irony in my words. By taking a student for the first time in over a century, I was indeed setting up the end of my story and the beginning of hers. "Death is merely another state of being. In the last moments of life, most pass on to one place or another, ending one phase of their existence and beginning the next. However, an aspect of the person they were remains on this plane, an echo if you will. Those like you and I have the ability to find that echo, magnify it, and bring sound from silence. Light from darkness."

"Life from death," she whispered.

"A step too far, Sullivan. None may return life to the dead, lest you believe the ancient scriptures contained in the holy books that pepper this world. We allow the dead to speak, to move, to act, but always remember, you speak not with the person, but their echo."

"But the robin," she said, recalling the first time she experienced the power that lived in both of us. "It flew away." Her face flushed. "It... breathed."

"A fluke. Perhaps the bird you held wasn't dead, but merely stunned."

"I know what I saw," she said. "What I felt."

Even then, on our first day, I saw it. The look of derision. The condescending moral superiority in her eyes that colored our every interaction. What she said was impossible. Truly returning life to the dead? A myth held closely by religions on every continent, true, but nothing I've ever encountered in my centuries walking the back alleys of this world. To see such a young soul claim to possess such power caused my blood to boil. Still, I couldn't turn her away. She reminded of… someone.

Plus, what if she was right?

"Be that as it may…" I didn't complete my thought that day, and even now, I don't know what more I would have or even could have said.

Now, this mere slip of a girl, my once apprentice, has destroyed my talisman, buried the empty husk that was once my body in hallowed ground, and forgotten me.

Mute.

Castrated.

And worst of all, forced to watch moments like this.

"The symphony?" A smile blossoms across Sullivan's world-weary face. The flicker of the candle at the center of the table reflects in her glistening eyes.

"Box seats." The constable I nearly ended in our grand confrontation at Arlington pulls a pair of tickets from his pocket and places them in Sullivan's outstretched palm. She's been seeing this man McLaren in the months since our battle, when one of the risen soldiers who should have been in my thrall instead ended me with a blade I carried at my side for over three hundred years. Since my essence now seems somehow tied to hers, I've been privy to every nausea-inducing moment of their courtship. I've pondered if Sullivan herself or the crescent of jade and platinum I fashioned for her holds my ruined soul close like iron filings to a magnet. She never strays far from the talisman though, nor the Janus dagger I placed in her charge.

Another mistake. Taking a student is one thing. Arming them with one of the few weapons in existence that can destroy you, another altogether. But things looked so promising in those days.

"The Janus dagger?" she asked me all those years ago.

"One of thirteen weapons forged over the centuries known as the Elder Blades. That weapon you hold is neither the most powerful of the set nor the least. Still, in matters of things not of this world, the dagger of Janus will serve you well."

Sullivan handled the weapon so very delicately that first time. "Janus. The two-headed god, right?"

"One set of eyes to look ahead and one to look behind. The god of passages and doorways, beginning and endings, his name immortalized in the word January, when winter begins its inexorable march toward spring."

Understanding flashed in her eyes. "Life from death."

"Yes, Sullivan. A most fitting weapon for a necromancer."

"But why give it to me?" she asked. "I don't plan to fight anyone. I only come here to understand what this power is that lives inside me, not to become a soldier."

She was so naïve back then.

"Sometimes, Sullivan, regardless of whether you choose to fight, the fight chooses you."

I pressed the hilt into her palm and gazed upon the phosphorescent sheen coming off the metal. Jealous, I remembered when the Elder Blade had served me, a power I enjoyed until the day I shed the wrong blood with its razor edge and its power was lost to me forever.

In our months together, I passed to Sullivan the wisdom of centuries, gave her a weapon of no small potency, even instructed her in its use, and in doing so, placed the instrument of my destruction in her tender hand.

The student truly becomes the teacher, I suppose. Isn't that how that tired old platitude goes?

When she sleeps. I fantasize about wrapping my hands around that lithe little neck of hers. When she walks the streets, I muse about pushing her out into traffic. And when she's with this man who helped end me? I imagine gutting him with the very blade I placed in her hand that day. I'd make her look on helpless as the light left his eyes before doing the same to her so I could enjoy the same.

But for now I merely watch. Without sleep, for I have no body that needs rest and without blinking, for I have no eyelids.

No eyes.

No anything.

Damn her.

"Shall we?" Sullivan rises from the table. After a quick kiss, she and her lover head for the door and as with every other time since I entered this hell-state between death and life, I am forced to follow.

The two of them saunter down the street, oblivious to the fact their every movement is being watched. They're pathetically happy. Young love. There is nothing quite like it.

And nothing more painful to lose.

Even the agony of the Janus blade skewering my heart came in a distant second to the torment of love lost forever.

I hadn't thought of Adelaide for years until these last months, but watching Sullivan and her lover has brought back memories I thought long buried. Adelaide's crystal blue eyes beneath her lustrous black tresses. Her supple skin without blemish. Her full lips that required no adornment. I let out a silent chuckle. Women of this millennium spend millions of dollars every year trying to capture the beauty Adelaide possessed every morning when she simply opened her eyes to the new day.

And she was mine.

"Julian," Adelaide said as we rode through the streets of London. "Do you love me?"

"More than life itself."

I glanced into her face, expecting to find a smile and an embarrassed blush. Instead, I found the strange disbelieving stare that had first crept onto her face a few weeks before.

"Don't be silly." Adelaide, who never bothered to learn how to ride sidesaddle, adjusted herself atop her steed. Her emerald green dress shimmered, the silk from which it was fashioned worth more than I had earned in my entire life to that point. "You would brave death for me?"

"I would." I pulled my horse closer to hers as we passed a narrow section along the cobblestone street. "I'd face a thousand deaths before I let any harm befall you."

"A thousand deaths?" she asked. "It would seem you've been attending a few too many of those silly plays over at the Globe. Your tongue's as glib as any of Mr. Shakespeare's actors' as they cavort about the stage."

"Glib, you say?" I can only imagine the affront borne upon my features in that moment. "You doubt my word?"

"Julian, Julian…" she sighed. "I doubt not for a minute that you believe yourself sincere in your grand proclamations of love. I've known you for the better part of a year, and though you are many things, a flatterer you are not."

"Then why do you mock me so?"

"I do not mock you, but I do wonder sometimes if you've considered fully some of the claims you make in the heat of passion."

A new voice came from behind us, deep and rough with

a harsh, guttural accent flavoring every word. "A man will say many things to charm a woman out of her bodice."

I spun in my saddle to confront whoever would dare interrupt my conversation with Adelaide and imply such motivation in my words. I may not have looked like much in my youth, but even then, the power was there. Nowhere near as strong or as refined as my abilities would one day become, but present. In any case, the corpulent fool riding behind us atop a mid-sized quarter horse had no idea who he was dealing with.

Or so I thought.

"Pardon me, sir," I asked, "but do I know you?"

"No, lad, but after following you and your lady friend the last half mile, I know you."

"And what might you mean by that, sir?"

"You, young man, are all tongue and swagger. I know your type. You build yourself up with words, like a peacock showing its plumage, but you don't have the berries to back it up."

Heat rose in my cheeks. "Take that back."

"Or what?" he asked. "You'll die the first of a thousand deaths to honor your lover?"

The pit of my stomach filled with cold anger. "She is not my lover."

"My apologies, lad," he said. "The lady was working to make that point just a moment ago."

"Please, sir," Adelaide interjected. "That's quite enough. We've done you no harm, so I would appreciate it if you'd leave us be."

"Well, that, you see, is where we have a problem." The plethoric stranger kicked at his horse's flanks and pulled his steed between Adelaide's and mine. "You see, your glib-tongued companion owes my employer a fair amount of money and I've been sent to collect."

"Of whom do you speak?" I asked, knowing full well who had sent him.

The man turned to me and smiled, inclining his head in a subtle bow. "Lord Worthington sends his regards."

"And why, pray tell, would Lord Worthington believe I owe him anything?" I returned the man's beatific smile. "He paid me for a service and that service has been provided."

"To your notion, perhaps," the stranger said. "My employer hired you to perform a very specific task, one you were not able to complete."

"Your employer wished to speak to his daughter again. I believe he got his wish."

"He wanted his daughter back, you dullard. You brought her back, let them speak, only to release her again into Death's embrace. How did you think he would react?"

"Death's embrace?" Fear filled Adelaide's voice as she reentered the conversation. "Of what does he speak, Julian?"

"She doesn't know?" Worthington's man rolled his eyes with glee. "How delightful."

I leaned into the man's space so that only he could hear my whisper. "Careful, now."

"Or what?" The man's fat face spread into a torturer's grin. "I have little doubt regarding your ability to usher a soul back from the grave, but I've heard nothing that leads me to believe you have the first idea of how to put one there."

"Julian," Adelaide said, "I'm frightened." She stopped her horse and pulled away into the shadow of a shopkeeper's awning.

I pulled my horse around the man's steed and placed myself between him and Adelaide. "You have nothing to fear from this man."

"It is not this man I fear, but the words he speaks. What

is all this talk of death and graves?"

"It is nothing."

The man took clear delight in my glare. "It is far from nothing, my dear. Tell me, are you familiar with the word 'necromancer'?" His fat grin grew even wider as Adelaide's confused stare leapt from the man to me.

"Julian," Adelaide said, "is it true? Are you one that deals in Death?"

"We can discuss this later when we are alone." I narrowed my eyes at the man. "Though, if this gentleman says one more word on the subject, he may need the services of such a person."

Worthington's man let out a laugh. "Come now, LaMorte. It's right there in the name you've chosen for yourself." Hearing him say my name aloud somehow made his threats all the more real. "Don't deny what you are, especially not to one who clearly means so much to you."

"Do not threaten us, sir." I turned my horse to face his and slid my rapier from its sheath. "And take care with the spouting of names. I would hate to be forced to cut your tongue from your head."

He let out a disappointed sigh. "Now you are embarrassing yourself. Put away your weapon and come with me or you will leave me no choice but to begin your lessons now."

"There is nothing you can teach me that I wish to learn." I brandished my weapon, to which the man clucked at the side of his cheek and drew his own. A dagger.

"You tread a narrow branch, LaMorte. Careful you don't take one step too many."

The dagger, hilt and all, was barely as long as the man's forearm, but I knew immediately this was no ordinary weapon. The blade glowed with an inner fire of blue and green, while the leather bound hilt met the base of the steel at a crosspiece fashioned into the two-headed bust of the Roman god, Janus.

To this day, I curse my arrogance. It wasn't Worthington's man who had no idea who he was dealing with, but me. Still, I had been embarrassed in front of the woman I loved and had no intention of backing down. I raised the tip of my rapier to the button that cinched the man's shirt closed at his collarbone. "You can tell your employer to rot in hell."

"Julian!" Adelaide screamed. "Do not antagonize the man."

"Oh, this has gone far beyond simple antagonism, sweet Adelaide." The man turned his toad grin back on her.

Adelaide's mouth dropped open. "You know even my name?"

Worthington's man offered her a condescending shrug. "Your names are but the least of what I know about the two of you."

"Leave her alone." The spark of fear at my core flared into full-blown flame. "You came here for me, did you not?"

"That bird has flown the cage, LaMorte." With a simple flick of his wrist, his glowing blade lopped off the tip of my sword. "We could have done this without causing your lady love any pain, but now…"

He slipped his free hand inside his coat and brought out a second object. If the dagger of Janus awakened in me some apprehension, the amulet he now held in his hand filled me with abject fear. I had only ever seen one of its kind before and bore the scars from the encounter.

"Sorcerer," I hissed.

"I prefer enchanter, Julian LaMorte, and I daresay that someone in your line of work has no business casting stones." He started a quiet murmur and the amulet answered with a pulsing drone and an inner golden light.

"What is he doing, Julian?" Adelaide pulled her horse close to mine, though her physical closeness only solidified the emotional distance that had sprung up between us. "And what is that thing he's holding?"

"Just stay behind me." I thrust at the man with my foreshortened rapier and he parried my blow without so much as a sideways glance. The remainder of my blade clattered to the ground, leaving me with no more than the haft of my weapon in my hand.

"What is this?" I asked, trying to keep any tremor from my voice. "Who are you?"

"Appellations are funny things, LaMorte, but as I long ago divorced myself from anything resembling a true name, you may call me Bindlekroff."

"Wait." Realization rushed through me like a torrent of water across a shattering dam. "Klaus Bindlekroff, the illusionist?"

His grin melted into a smug smirk. "It seems my reputation precedes me."

"Julian." Adelaide's voice grew low and full of trepidation. "Take me away from here."

I ignored her. As I always did when it was the most important.

I pulled close to the enchanter and whispered into his ear. "Mr. Bindlekroff, sir. My apologies. I had no idea to whom I was speaking."

"Clearly."

"We can make this right." I pulled him to one side. "I will leave with you now and speak to your employer, but with one condition."

His head tilted to the right as his eyes glazed over. "And

whatever might that be?"

"You must agree to teach me." Simple. Confident. To the point. And ultimately, my undoing.

"Oh," Bindlekroff said. "your lesson awaits, have no fear of that."

***

So many triumphs Sullivan owes to this chance meeting with the mysterious enchanter, Klaus Bindlekroff. Just two months past, she faced off against an old adversary of mine, the arch-demon Solomon. The amulet of illusions Bindlekroff lent her was all that let her close enough close enough to strike, and without a weapon like the Janus dagger, there's no doubt she would have died in the attempt. She has no idea what price I paid to carry that most undervalued of the Elder Blades. But I know the cost. I remember it well, and if I ever have opportunity to impart her with one last lesson, Sullivan will learn.

***

Bindlekroff raised the amulet above his head and fire erupted at our horses' feet. Fire that did not burn or scorch or even give off heat. As if the beasts beneath us could tell the difference. My horse reared, nearly sending me to the cobblestone street, as Adelaide's took off at a dead sprint.

"I would have come willingly," I screamed at Bindlekroff. "You didn't have to do this."

"Oh, but I did." He put away his bauble and cracked his knuckles. "When next we speak, I will have your undivided attention." His eyes followed the dust trail left by Adelaide's horse. "Best hurry, if you wish to catch her."

With one last glance at Bindlekroff, I spurred my horse and chased after Adelaide. Boxed in by the market on either side, the animal was easy to follow; however, a terrified horse running a straightaway is about as easy to catch as a falling star. I cursed my limited talents. Even then, I had more than enough power to raise a score of corpses to fight for me, controlling them all like choreographed marionettes. But stopping a runaway steed was another matter altogether.

"Adelaide," I shouted. "Jump!"

I'm not certain if she couldn't hear me over the roar of the hooves or if she was simply too scared to move, but Adelaide clung to the reins with all her might and didn't so much as look back at my repeated cries.

"Yah!" I spurred my horse again and with a sudden burst of speed, we closed the gap a few feet. No more than fifty yards separated us, but it may as well have been fifty miles. Given time, I would have eventually caught her. I had the more powerful horse, and with my slender build, I didn't outweigh Adelaide by more than a few pounds. Time however was not on my side.

Three streets south, the Thames awaited. Not far from where I laid my head at the time, that particular stretch of road I knew all too well terminated on a blind curve that had sent its fair share of pack animals into the river.

And none of those were panicked, fleeing a sorcerer's illusory flames.

"Come on, Hermes," I whispered to the horse. "Live up to your name." I drove the spurs again into the horse's flanks and closed the gap to twenty-five feet. Adelaide shot a hysterical glance back at me, her eyes wide and her skin as pale as the white steed that bore her. Another minute and I would have caught them, but it was a minute I didn't have. In the four hundred years since walking this Purgatory of a world, I have never again felt so helpless.

I made damn sure of that.

The horse darted around the corner and was out of sight for no more than a few seconds. I heard a tortured whinny followed by a blood-curdling scream extinguished a bit too early. I rounded the corner and found the horse rearing, its saddle empty, but Adelaide was nowhere in sight. The only other person present was a boy whose expression mirrored the terror I had seen in Adelaide's face just moments before.

"The woman," I screamed. "Where is she?"

Driven mute by what he had seen, the boy merely pointed at the river. Just beyond the horse's flailing form, the top rail was split as if hit by a sledgehammer, the jagged wood soaked in crimson. I leapt from the horse and ran to the fence. My finger traced the slick blood and found a clump of hair. Long. Curly. Black.

"No!" Gripping the fence, I leaned over and peered into the water. The river was particularly muddy from recent rainfall, as if the "Sewer Thames" was ever clear in those days. At first, I could find no sign of Adelaide, but as the current pushed one of the boats further downstream, I saw her. The green silk of her dress all but black in the muddy water, she floated face down just a few feet from the river's edge. Before I knew what I was doing, I was under the fence and scrambling down the riverbank. I still remember the foul taste of the river as I fell climbing in, the mouthful of mud, piss, and shit far from the bitterest medicine I'd taste that day. Like a half-drowned dog, I paddled over to Adelaide's still form and crooked an arm around her strangely turned neck. Pulling her behind me, I fought against the current and swam to a small dock a few yards downstream.

"You," yelled the dock's proprietor as I grasped at the ladder, "get away from there."

"You rat bastard," I screamed. "Can't you see? She's drowning."

He looked past me, and his scowl melted, at least a little. He tore off his coat, which I suspect cost more than I made in three months back then, and helped pull me and Adelaide up onto the floating wooden platform.

"What are you doing in the river, lad?"

Ignoring him, I flipped Adelaide onto her back, and did my best to ignore as well the open wound on the back of her skull.

"Please, Adelaide. Please don't die." Even as the words left my mouth, I knew what was going to happen. What I was going to do. "Not now."

"I'm sorry to tell you this, lad," the old man said, "but she's gone."

With one hand still on Adelaide's pulseless neck, I grasped the old man's collar. "She's gone when I say she's gone."

I'm not certain what passed my eyes in that moment. A flash of mystic fire? A hint of the Darkness? Or merely the rage welling up from the depths of my soul? Regardless, the man ran screaming from the pier as if he'd seen the Devil himself.

His assessment was not far from the mark.

"Now, Adelaide, you will see." I pulled a short blade from my boot and ran its blade across my palm, its razor edge leaving a trail of scarlet. Looking back, I have no idea why I was in such a hurry. A modern paramedic would have had only minutes to revive her, but when you bring the skills of a necromancer to bear, there is little difference between dead for minutes and dead for days. Still, in my flustered rush, I didn't take the usual precautions drilled into me by my own master. I didn't lay out a circle of containment, didn't use any words or sigils of control, didn't even cover myself with a protective charm. So desperate was I to bring her back, I ignored everything I had been taught. I rushed through the steps, smearing my lifeblood across her eyelids and lips, then laid my crimson-covered hands across her chest.

"And... breathe."

The rush of power that flowed through my hands was unlike any I'd felt before or since. Was the power I felt merely magnified by the sheer panic of the moment or in my desperation, had I indeed pulled from a deeper well?

A moment later, Adelaide opened her eyes, looked up at me, and smiled. At my command, the only woman I ever loved had returned to me and for a moment, all was again well with the world.

A fleeting moment.

"Julian?" she whispered, her voice like the creak of a rusty hinge. "What happened?"

"You fell in the river." I did my best to ignore the bits of grey matter floating like boats down the crimson river coursing from the gaping hole in her skull. "You were... hurt."

"Really?" She glanced to her left and right. "I don't feel anything."

"You hit your head." I pulled a soaked kerchief from my coat pocket and reached to dab at the open wound just above her left ear. "Here. Let me help you."

She stared at me for a moment more, her eyes already glazed, then glanced down at her dress. Its emerald hue muted by the mud and excrement of the river, a trail of maroon flowed down her neck, across her left breast, and down onto her overskirt.

"Is all this blood mine?" she asked.

I remembered the sheer terror in her eyes at the mere mention of the word "necromancer" and had no doubt as to her reaction when the reality of her death finally became clear.

"Julian? What have you done?"

"I did what I had to. I saved you."

"Saved me?" Her attention turned to her right arm, which was bent at far more places than just her elbow and wrist. "I'm bleeding like a slaughtered pig, the bones of my arm are shattered and I feel none of it."

"I…" I had no idea what to say. The truth would send her over the edge and Adelaide was far too sharp to believe a lie. Her strength of mind was one of the many things I loved about her.

"You… you raised me." The fire returned to her waterlogged gaze. "What that horrible man said about you. It was true."

"I brought you back." I took her cold fingers in my hand. "So that we could be together. Don't you see?"

Her eyes narrowed. "You knew how I felt about all of this. What you do. What you are. How could you do this to me, Julian? Return me to this mockery of life?" Her open hand whipped out like a viper and struck me across the face. "What of my immortal soul? Did you consider that, oh great and powerful necromancer?" She spat the words as if they were the foulest insult she could muster.

"I couldn't bear losing you."

"If you had left me dead, there is a chance we would have eventually found each other in the realm beyond, but in doing what you have done, you have lost me. For ever and ever."

Before I could say another word, she sprinted from the pier, up the bank, and headed back into the narrow streets and alleys of London proper. Between the trail of blood and the screams, she was quite easy to follow, though her fury gave her speed beyond anything I would have imagined possible. She led me for quite the chase, but when I finally caught up to her, I found her standing with one pale hand on her hip, patiently awaiting my arrival.

Looking back now, her destination should never have been in any doubt.

"See, Julian?" she said as she stepped past the wide-eyed blacksmith and into the heat of his forge. "See what you have driven me to?" Not an ounce of pain showed on her face as the flames swept up her body.

"I'm sorry." Tears filled my eyes. Not the first time I ever cried, but definitely the last. "I only did what I did because I love you."

"What you have for me," she hissed, her dead skin splitting and turning black in the heat, "is selfishness. Pride. Lust. But love? You don't know the meaning of the word."

"But…" Before I could complete my thought, she fell into the flames and her entire form was engulfed in seconds. I felt an obligation to watch her immolation clear to the end as one final measure of respect but even in that, I failed, as my thoughts quickly turned to revenge.

"Bindlekroff."

I raced back to the crossing where I'd left the enchanter thinking in my pride he would have fled my wrath but was unpleasantly surprised to find he hadn't moved an inch.

"Ah, LaMorte. You have returned so soon. Are you really so eager to begin your tutelage?"

"I want nothing from you but your death."

"That couldn't be farther from the truth, and both you and I know it. Come. Let us go discuss the matter at hand with Lord Worthington, then you and I can continue your training."

"Continue?"

"Why, yes, LaMorte." That toad grin of his returned for an encore presentation. "You've already had your first lesson from me, perhaps the most important of all."

"And what would that be, enchanter?" I spat the words at him.

"That everything dies." His sneer fills me with bile. "Friends. Enemies. Lovers. Everything, that is, but power." He passed his amulet from one hand to another. "Be it passed on, lost, found, rediscovered, power is forever. Do you understand?"

The white-hot flame at my core flared, but I kept the fire from my eyes. "You truly expect me to follow you after what you've done?"

"I expect nothing, necromancer. I simply know where your black heart truly lies."

"I loved her, you bastard."

"And if you loved her more than you loved power, we wouldn't be having this conversation." Bindlekroff clasped my shoulder in a firm grip. It was akin to being caressed by a serpent. "A couple things you will quickly learn about me, LaMorte. In matters pertaining to a man's nature, I am never wrong."

"And the other?" I asked.

He smiled grimly. "My lessons may be harsh, but they are not easily forgotten."

Despite the hatred rushing through my veins, I became Bindlekroff's student that day. I joined him with the simple intention of getting close enough to exact my revenge when the moment presented itself. But days became weeks, months, years. When we finally parted ways at the end of my apprenticeship, Adelaide's smile had become a distant memory. Only now, watching Sullivan and her lover standing huddled close on a city street corner, does the pain return. A lesson from my once apprentice that one thing other than power never dies.

Regret.

"Care to come back to my place?" Sullivan's eyebrow rises as a subtle smile plays across her lips.

"Sounds good, but I've got an early morning." He pulls her even closer. "All right if I stay?"

"Of course." She pulls his face down to hers in a passionate kiss. "Truth be told, the shower seems kind of empty in the morning without you."

In that moment, I'm grateful that whatever curse has left me as Sullivan's invisible one-man entourage at least allows me to look away. And that's when I see it.

Impending murder, and less than half a minute away.

A bus hurtles toward the intersection as the lights go yellow. A balding man in a long black overcoat checks his smartphone, oblivious to the bruiser in the dark tracksuit and sunglasses standing behind him. Sunglasses, with the sun dropping below the horizon half an hour ago. Half a second before the bus reaches the corner, the man in the overcoat falls into the street. Tires squall. People scream. A little girl cries.

And blood flows.

Sullivan and the constable race to the corner, my once apprentice to the injured man's side and her lover after the man in the tracksuit and shades. Sullivan cradles the man's head in her lap. Such caring in her eyes. The years will drive the tenderness from her heart as surely as they drove it from mine. Still, it burns now, seeing her so confident in her self-righteousness.

As if she has something I never did.

A crowd begins to form, the passersby drawing closer and closer, threatening to suffocate her until Sullivan's lover returns and disperses the mob. As he singles out in particular the ones with cameras, I can all but see what's going on behind that no-nonsense grimace.

"All right, April. We're clear." The constable leans beside her. "Can you help him?"

She glances up, frustration etched in her features. "He's still alive, Gavin."

"So?" He whips off his belt and wraps it around the man's bleeding thigh. "Can't you at least stabilize him till the paramedics can get here?"

"What part of necromancer don't you understand?" Her voice comes out as a sharp hiss, a tone I've rarely if ever heard her use with this man. It's like music to my ears. "As much as I want to help, mystical first aid is a little outside of my purview."

"But I thought it was 'all just energy.' Isn't that what you always say?"

"I've never brought my abilities to bear against someone who hadn't already…" Her voice grows quiet. "…you know, passed on."

"The man just got hit by a bus. I don't think you can mess him up any worse."

"Things can always be worse." A grim smile invades Sullivan's face. "Trust me."

Adelaide's pale face flashes again across my memory. She's right. It can always be worse.

The man breathing goes agonal, gasping labored inspirations followed by frothy, blood-tinged coughs. He stands on Death's door, and I would know. I've stood in its open doorway for months.

"It's now or never, April."

I honestly don't know which impresses me more: the constable's utter conviction that he is right in his belief or his complete ignorance of how far he is out of his league even discussing such matters.

And then, going against everything I ever taught her, Sullivan does the unthinkable. She fishes her talisman from her purse, its grey metal coruscating with a green shimmer.

Puncturing her thumb with its sharp tip, she traces a streak of scarlet across each eyelid, then across his lips before slipping the crescent of platinum and jade under the man's shirt

She utters a single word.

"Breathe."

The ether surrounding us ripples outward from her talisman as if a boulder has been thrown into a placid lake. She can clearly feel it, but I can see it, in this in-between place to which I've been sentenced. Power fills the air, washing over me, around me, through me.

And suddenly, I'm somewhere else. And not just that.

I'm someone else.

My head lies in Sullivan's lap and I find myself staring up into those insightful blue eyes of hers. For the first time in my memory, I find neither hate nor disdain there, but compassion.

"Sir," she whispers. "Can you hear me?"

"Yes." And not the strange half-telepathic whispering that I've been forced to endure for the last several months. I hear her. The sensation of actual sound hitting my ears is intoxicating.

Though the ears are not exactly mine.

"What's your name?" Sullivan asks.

My mouth begins to form a lie, that I have no memory of my name, that the blow has rendered me amnesiac, but then I realize a strange and terrible truth. I do know my name.

"I'm Jack." It's neither my name nor my voice. "Jack Peterson."

"Well, Jack Peterson. You are one lucky man."

She has no idea.

"I don't feel so lucky." A glance down reveals this Jack Peterson's arm bent at a strange angle at the midpoint between his elbow and wrist. Bony fragments like jagged teeth erupt from the flesh there and the pool of blood on the asphalt grows wider by the second. Still, even the agony coursing through every inch of this body is a thousand times better than the absence of sensation that has for months been my reality.

A reality brought on by this woman who now cradles my head between her warm thighs. It's all but poetic, the symmetry.

What I plan to do to her, not as much.

"You've been injured," the constable says, "but the paramedics are on the way." He kneels by my side and grasps my uninjured hand. His fingers are warm against my anemic palm. "But I think you're going to be all right."

"Yes, constable." I squeeze his fingers with every ounce of strength I can muster. "It would seem I'm going to be just fine."

# AUTHOR'S NOTE

"Have you ever thought about writing a story about a necromancer?"

In the summer of 2009, I had been in Charlotte less than a year and had fallen in with a dangerous crowd.

You guessed it.

Writers.

All of them.

As we gathered around the table at one of our favorite watering holes (of the caffeinated variety), my friend, Eden, announced that a small press that specialized in horror fiction was accepting submissions for a necromancer-based anthology. At the time, I was working on edits for my first novel, a contemporary fantasy, and had never considered writing another horror story after the less than rave reviews my story "Grim Tidings" received in the short story contest my senior year of high school. But Eden seemed excited to explore this genre as did our mutual friend, Matthew, and as it happened, the three of us all ended up getting into the anthology. Pill Hill Press's *Flesh and Bone: Rise of the Necromancers* was for each of us our first publication, and what made it even sweeter was the fact that we were all in the same anthology together. Since then, the three of us, along with others in our group, have continued to publish and even share pages again on more than one occasion, but the heady excitement of seeing your name on the page as "author" for the first time is one that is hard to top.

My first story ended with a twist that M. Night Shyamalan would be proud of—and yes, I remember when that was a good thing. The POV character may or may not be a bit of a necro*philiac*—I leave that to the reader's imagination—but the necro*mancer* of the story is actually the supposed damsel in distress, a character who ended up becoming my titular necromancer for hire. Reading it in this format, as an April Sullivan collection, the bite this story is supposed to have and the jarring surprise I intended at the end are both a bit lost, but I still stand behind this story as a fun tale of turning the tables and a fine introduction to one of my favorite characters.

I never intended to write about April again after that story, but various calls for submissions continued to pop up where the lovely Miss Sullivan seemed to fit right in. From sibling rivalry with a vampire brother to the inevitable story of student facing master to the true horror of a loved one's funeral to the literal facing of one's demons to my little version of the worst date ever and ending with the resurrection of our hero's greatest foe, April and I have had a fun few years. Other projects have taken my attention, but in the doldrums between novels, April often tells me another story.

And when April talks, I listen.

Never fear. The last story in this book is not the end of April's adventures by any stretch of the imagination. I know where she's headed next and what she must face, and when that story is ready to come, it will come. Till then, enjoy this collection. I know I've enjoyed creating it.

***

April Sullivan's first three tales initially appeared in the following anthologies from the now defunct Pill Hill Press: *Flesh and Bone: Rise of the Necromancers*, *Monster Mash*, and *Dark Heroes*, while her fifth, "Solomon," initially appeared in *The Big Bad: An Anthology of Evil* from Dark Oak Press. "Class Reunion," "Symphony of Wolves," and "The Fall and Rise of Julian

LaMorte" are unique to this collection and together round out her initial seven stories.

\*\*\*

The story "Class Reunion" is dedicated to the memory of Phillip Leonard, a friend from high school, college, and Scouts. We all miss you Phil.

\*\*\*

Special thanks to Roy Mauritsen for the brilliant cover design as well as the distinctive interior layout of this book. Without him, my Necromancer for Hire would likely be out of a job. An accomplished writer and graphic designer himself, Roy's fairy tale adventure series, *Shards of the Glass Slipper*, is available from Padwolf Publishing. Find him online at roymauritsen.com.

\*\*\*

April Sullivan will return, her next story a novella (or perhaps, a novel…) that is still gestating in Darin's twisted little mind with a working title of *29 Days*.

# ABOUT THE AUTHOR

Darin Kennedy, born and raised in Winston-Salem, North Carolina, is a graduate of Wake Forest University and Bowman Gray School of Medicine. After completing family medicine residency in the mountains of Virginia, he served eight years as a United States Army physician and wrote his first novel in 2003 in the sands of northern Iraq. His debut novel, The Mussorgsky Riddle, was  born from a fusion of two of his lifelong loves, classical music and world mythology, and was released January 2015 from Curiosity Quills Press. His short stories, including some found in this very collection, can be found in various anthologies and magazines and he is currently hard at work on several new projects. Doctor by day and novelist by night, he writes and practices medicine in Charlotte, North Carolina. When not engaged in either of the above activities, he has been known strum the guitar, enjoy a bite of sushi, and rumor has it he even sleeps on occasion. He is represented by Stacey Donaghy at Donaghy Literary Group. Find him online at darinkennedy.com.

Made in the USA
Monee, IL
02 June 2021